Theta Corps

CONTRITION

ALIYAH BURKE

Contrition
ISBN # 978-1-78686-332-4
©Copyright Aliyah Burke 2017
Cover Art by Posh Gosh ©Copyright October 2017
Interior text design by Claire Siemaszkiewicz
Totally Bound Publishing

Published in 2017 by Totally Bound Publishing, Think Tank, Ruston Way, Lincoln, LN6 7FL, United Kingdom.

CONTRITION

Dedication

To DH, thank you for all you do for me. I love you!

Chapter One

"Let me get this straight, you let her go off with this jackass named Carlos, who isn't only strictly an ex, but her ex-*husband*?"

Masters strode back and forth in front of his desk, raking a hand through his dark hair. He'd never wanted to hurt the ones in this room so much in his entire life. There were two men in his office with him — two of his best, but for the moment he wanted nothing more than to beat them to death for allowing this to happen. Ethan and Beau Jackson didn't look any happier than he was, but still. It was different.

"She didn't give us any choice, Masters," Ethan commented. "You know damn well Anabelle Lee doesn't *let* anyone tell her what she can or can't do."

While the man was still thin from his confinement and torture but had improved all the way around. It had no hope of saving him from getting his ass beat, given the mood Masters was in. Masters crossed his arms and sat on the edge of his desk. "How do you figure?"

He cocked an eyebrow and gave Masters a 'duh' look. "Because she told us she would go and we couldn't stop her."

New anger surged to life within him. The moment he got her back, he was going to bend her over his knee and spank her. *That is fun on an entirely new level. And it will do something for our relationship.*

"I think she has plans to take him down. She wanted us out of the way. You know how his sister gets when she's pissed off. Plus, they tried to strip search her at the palace and it still irked her. When he showed up on the scene, we both knew that man was going to get the brunt of her anger." Beau stretched his legs and hooked his cowboy boots at the ankle. Of the three gathered in the room, he quite honestly didn't appear concerned about what his cousin had gotten herself into. Masters wasn't too sure what to make of it.

Then again, perhaps my reaction is completely unprofessional of me.

Masters stared at the cousins, eyes flicking back and forth between them like a ping-pong ball used in a championship match. "I want her found and brought back. We went through this already after you were taken, Ethan. I can't keep having my agents kidnapped."

"No offense, Masters, but I also wish my sister back home. Not just your agent. But *our* family."

"Keep me posted." He stood and hollered for his secretary. "Mino!"

"Right here."

He exhaled and held out his hand for the papers she carried in. "What are these?" His words were sharp.

Mino didn't appear at all affected. "Basic things that need to be signed. I haven't heard from Anabelle Lee as of yet but will let you know when her phone comes back online or we hear from her." She looked to the cousins. "Ethan, Beau."

Masters carried the stack to his desk and signed them all with a flurry, not paying a lick of attention to what was there. He didn't mind. He trusted Mino with everything. Scrubbing a hand over his head, he cracked his neck and looked at the woman picking up the papers.

"What?"

She glared right back at him, obviously unimpressed by the scowl on his face. That was part of why he liked her so much—she wasn't timid around him. "Don't bark at me just because she didn't ask for your permission to do what she had to in order to help save her family."

"Excuse me?" He leaned back in the black leather chair.

"You heard me fine." She stated walking to the door, not bothering to look back in his direction. "I'm not here for you to fight with. While I have many job duties, that is not one. If that's what you need, call upon Ethan or Beau and take one of them to the mat."

She vanished before he said anything else. The two men in the room had smiles they wiped from their face the moment he glared back at them.

"Any takers?"

It didn't surprise him in the least when Beau stepped forward. The man loved hand-to-hand combat and took any and all opportunities to increase his knowledge of it.

"Not me," Ethan said, holding out his hands as he shook his head. "I'm going home to my princess, then I'm going to start tracking down my sister."

"Let me know when you get a hit." Beau made the comment without moving toward the door.

"Always."

Ethan slipped from view. Masters rested his hands on the desktop and looked at the man in his office.

"She'll be fine, Masters."

"At least until I get my hands on her," he growled. However, that was a double-edged sword for him. He coveted Anabelle Lee in ways he hadn't any right to. She worked for him.

Not that his being in a position of power would be an issue for her. Hell, most of the time she defied orders, anyway. All he knew was that when she stood next to him, warmth swallowed him. He could smell her skin and longed to bury his face in her thick red tresses.

God, he wanted her hair of liquid flame streaming over him while they were in bed, limbs entwined. He held his breath and strove to keep his emotions under control. The woman was all fire and ice. She was his weak link — the chink in his armor. *Lord help me if she ever figures that out.*

He allowed this group of Theta Corps operatives a lot more leeway than he did other teams. They were his best group and yet he couldn't help but think of the issues they'd had over the past few years.

"Stop blaming yourself."

He snapped his head up to find Beau helping himself to the scotch sitting on the sideboard.

At least he's pouring two.

"What makes you think I'm blaming myself?" He accepted the drink and took a healthy swallow, relishing the burn.

"Because I know you. You still blame yourself for what happened to Valentino and Lexy."

"It's my job to keep you safe so you in turn can keep the world safe."

"Nothing is safe anymore, Masters." He lowered himself into a chair and rested one booted foot over the opposite knee. "We do the job because we believe in it. We do it for you because we trust you. Ethan doesn't blame you — *we* don't blame you for Anabelle Lee. Hell, even Valentino doesn't blame you. So you're the only one — "

"Beauregard!"

Masters looked to the doorway on the heels of the frustrated roar coming from Mino's desk.

"Her dulcet tones," he drawled, pushing to his feet. "I do so love to hear her calling my name." After finishing his drink, he sauntered from the office, moving as if he hadn't a care in the world. As if Mino hadn't spat his name with the heat of a thousand suns or the chill of the coldest winter.

Masters got about two sentences before the door slammed and he couldn't hear them bicker any longer. He rubbed his temples and wished he was home.

Ain't all I wish. I want that woman home where she belongs.

Masters did a bit more work then rose to his feet. He walked to the coat rack he hung his black leather coat on each morning and pulled it free. He slipped into it as he exited his office and found Mino wasn't at her desk. Her things were still there so he knew she couldn't have left yet.

"Mino?" he called out, digging for his truck keys.

"In the copy room fixing the printer."

He headed to where she was and stuck his head into the room. "What happened to it?"

"Beau."

He rolled his eyes. "The two of you need to work out this issue you have with each another."

"There's no issue," she snapped. "I'm just tired of him thinking I'm his secretary here to take all the messages from the whores he fucks." She jerked on the paper, ripping it free.

Really, what does one say in response to that? "Do you want me to talk to him?"

"God, no!" She jerked her head up and looked at him, an apologetic expression on her face taking place of the stress and anger previously there. "I'm sorry, I don't mean it that way. Just if he thinks I run to the boss because I'm not happy he's only going to annoy me further. It's his way. He gets under my skin is all."

Yeah, and in ways you may not even want to acknowledge. "If you're sure. But if you change your mind, I'm more than happy to let him know you're my secretary."

She slammed the door shut on the copier and snarled at him. "I believe the politically correct term is administrative assistant."

This was one reason he had her, besides the fact that she was damn amazing at her job—she made him smile. And, on occasion, laugh.

"I stand corrected."

She crumpled the papers in her hand and cocked an eyebrow in his direction. "You do realize I make your coffee in the morning. And I know all your drinks. Working around the lot of you, I've learned more than I should on how to kill someone."

"Noted." He sobered. "I'm heading out. Are you ready to go?"

She shook her head. "I've got a bit more to handle. Don't worry, I will be fine."

He hated leaving her alone in the building, regardless of the fact that it was safe. Masters shook his head. "I'll just do more in my office and leave when you do."

"No, you have things to do tonight. I would have been done but with Beau's women interfering in my job, I am behind."

"Okay, then." He whipped out his phone and called Beau.

"Masters?"

"You need to come to the office and wait for Mino to finish so she has an escort to walk her out. She's behind because of the messages from your women." He ended the call before Beau complained. "I'll wait until he gets here, then I'll head home."

She walked past him and squeezed his arm. "You do realize just how secure this building is, right? I'm perfectly safe in here."

He viewed her as his little sister. The one female in his life he trusted not to break his heart. She had her past and he didn't care — they all did. She was one of his now and he would keep her safe.

"Are you telling me to leave?"

"Yes." Her word was succinct and instant.

"You know who's the boss, right?"

"I know who thinks they are and who truly runs this place. Go home, I'll be fine."

He debated but left as soon as Beau sent him a text that he was in the building. The drive home was quiet. He didn't even turn on the radio. His mind swarmed with the possibilities of what Anabelle Lee could be going through. "Damn her for making me worry."

He pulled into his garage and climbed out of his truck. He unzipped his jacket as he walked into the house and drew the door shut behind him. A warning tingle ran up his spine, and within seconds he had his VP9 Tactical in hand.

He cleared each room in silence as he worked his way to his bedroom. He paused outside the door before bursting in, ready to fire at whatever may be facing him.

Blinking the sleep away but holding a Walther PPK on him with unwavering steadiness was none other than Anabelle Lee. Her red hair streamed forward, messy and sexy, only partially covering the bruise on her light tan skin.

"What the fuck are you doing in my house?" he demanded, eyes widening as he lowered his sidearm. "And where the hell have you been?"

She rested her gun on the mattress. Her blue eyes homed in on him and a slight quirk of her lips went straight to his groin.

"Not asking me what I'm doing in your bed?"

He cocked his head to the left and lifted his right eyebrow. His chest burned and his stomach clenched as he struggled to regain control. His brain raced to form a sentence that wouldn't come out as, 'If you're in my house of your own accord, I would assume you to be in my bed, for that's the place I plan on keeping you.'

"Let's start with you answering my questions."

Anabelle Lee ignored the overwhelming stiffness in her body — made worse from her unexpected slumber — and glided from the bed. No, correction, not *the* bed, *his* bed. As in belonging to her boss, Masters. Ever attentive, all seeing, and the one man she wanted in a way that was less than professional. She had no desire for her boss to get a bead on just how truly sore she was.

Truth be told, she'd had intentions of being awake when he arrived back to his place, but five seconds on his large bed and she'd pretty much fallen unconscious. It didn't hurt that she was surrounded by a combination of warmth and his scent.

"I *am* waiting, Anabelle Lee."

The fury lining his tone, barely contained, sent fissures of warning throughout her body. His black eyes were hard as obsidian.

"Your place was closer." There had been a time when she would have deepened her drawl and flirted, but not with Masters. Theirs was a different relationship.

Business only. No matter what her body might be in favor of sharing with him.

"Still no reason for you to be here, much less in my bed."

She approached him, just slowly enough to mask her sore and injured body. Halting before him, she exhaled one long breath as her gaze locked onto his.

"I didn't interrupt anything because you don't bring women home with you. So why the anger? My brother and Beau, I get, but you? I'm an employee who is back fine. Unless you're mad you weren't in your bed *with* me."

His nostrils flared, but that was the only reaction aside from the clenching of his squared jaw. *Okay, perhaps not strictly business, because I do love getting these reactions from him.*

"Is that it? You wondering if I'm a true redhead?" She smiled. *So much for boss-employee lines, because I just jumped way over them.* "Only a few know the truth. Good night. You know where to find me if you want the answer to that."

Without looking back, she continued her slow trek out of the door and onward to the elevator. Once the silver doors slid closed behind her she allowed the wince to cross her face. Beads of sweat had gathered on her forehead and with an angry swipe she dashed them away.

I hate feeling weak. "Shit, I hurt. He's right. I should have gone straight home."

However, she wouldn't have made it home. She still had nearly to an hour and a half to make it to her property and personal bed. When'd she broken into his place, she'd been bruised and still bleeding.

Now I'm just bruised.

She also had avoided home because her family would know and be at her place playing twenty questions. She just needed sleep. Anabelle Lee wriggled her toes, welcomed the pain and schooled her emotions to give nothing away the moment the elevator doors slid back open, allowing her to walk out.

A hotel room. That was her first order of business. *I can't check in under my name or any of my aliases. Those will pop to my family, as well.* And she had no doubt her brother had each one flagged.

And she wasn't about to recover in a hellhole. There were cash reserves and weapon stashes she could access. That would, however, take more energy than she had.

She left Masters' house, withdrawing her phone as she went. As she waited for a cab ride, she placed another call.

"Hello?" The woman on the other end had a deep, southern drawl.

"I need your help, Lexy."

A brief moment of silence. "Red?"

Anabelle Lee bristled over the name. This was the only woman—hell, the only person—who called her that.

"Has hell frozen over? I didn't think it had, yet you are calling me and asking for help."

Anabelle Lee waved at a nearing taxi. "A simple yes or no is all I need."

"Of course, I'll help. It's got to be serious if you're calling me over Val."

Lexy's husband Valentino Casanno was a man she'd worked with on numerous occasions. She actually liked the man but she and Lexy went together about as nice as oil and water. She'd never call them friends. And that was the precise reason she called her. No one would think she would reach out to Lexy for help of disappearing.

"I need a hotel room rented for me."

"I can book one for you under our clinic. Since it will be under us, I'll still be able to use your name. If that works for you."

She wobbled on her feet as she approached the idling vehicle. "That would be fine. I can't use any of my own cards, but I will—"

"Don't worry about it. How long do you need it for?"

"A week."

A slight grunt. "Give me a moment."

Typing came over the line as she settled into the back of the cab.

"Where to?" the driver questioned.

"I'm making hotel arrangements, head downtown please." She made sure to alter her voice, there was no southern accent at all. Right now, she sounded like someone who'd grown up in Boston. Even that minor adjustment was a huge feat for her and took more of her wanning energy.

Exhaustion nipped at her heels as she gave one-word responses to Lexy, who had to figure out where she was and what hotel to get her to. Once the hotel had been booked, she sighed.

"Thank you."

"Sure thing, Red." Lexy hung up.

Passing along the name of the hotel, she fought the sleep weighing on her. Even near collapse, she didn't let down her guard until she set the locks on the door to the suite. She'd hung the *Do Not Disturb* sign on the door.

After another shower that sapped her remaining strength, she staggered to the bed, wrapped in a large white robe. Perched on the edge, she hung her head and reached for the Walther PPK beside her.

She might have been about to crash for a while but she wasn't an idiot. She never slept without a weapon. She ensured it had a full magazine before she stuffed it under a large pillow on the bed and crawled in with only a long shirt on, after having shed her robe on the chair nearby. Generally, she slept on her side but right now, on her back was how it was going to have to be.

Once she was situated, she slipped her left hand beneath the pillow with her sidearm and curved her hand around the butt. Then she allowed herself to succumb to exhaustion.

* * * *

Anabelle Lee slept for two days before she felt better. Using the hotel phone, she called down for room service as checked she made sure her cell battery was still out of the device so her family couldn't trace her. Some days, it sucked to work for an agency that tended to be able to find its operatives no matter where they went or what they did.

She prayed that going through Lexy would buy her the time she needed to recover. After hanging up from the front desk, she padded into the large bathroom and turned on the shower. Once the steam began filling the space she removed her nightshirt and stepped into the tub, groaning in ecstasy as the heated pellets pounded her skin. Mindful of her healing injuries, she didn't scrub too hard on some spots, and it took her a while to wash her hair, but she stepped out, feeling much better.

Although more sleep wouldn't be a bad thing.

She reached for a fresh robe, which sat folded up in the room, and let it unfold then slipped it on. Hair secured by a towel, she put on her socks and went back out to the main room of the suite. With an eye on the time, so she was dressed when room service arrived, she decided she needed to get a bit of shopping done. It wouldn't do to wear the same thing the whole week. Although she was going to be doing a lot more sleeping.

She had just pulled on her jeans and hung her long shirt over the blood on the blue denim when a knock came. A final glance at the mirror showed nothing more than an exhausted woman with wet hair. She palmed the Walther and walked to the door.

Swinging it open, she waved the man in. It didn't take him long to wheel in the trolley and while he was setting it up, she moved closer to him.

"Here you are."

"Thank you." She signed the slip with her right hand and walked with him to the door. "Have a nice day."

His smile was kind, then he was gone. She uncovered the food and the rich smells had her mouth watering. She was starving.

Sitting at the table, she picked up the fork and prepared to dig into the omelet on the plate before her when the itch reappeared between her shoulder blades. She rose from the table and paused before she crept toward the bedroom part of the suite.

The door was as she'd left it, open and cracked about an inch. No way someone had come in through the window, so that wasn't it. Were Ethan with her, he would have kicked in the door to keep the element of surprise.

He wasn't. She only had the Walther on her. The rest of her weapons resided in the room she stood outside of. Peeking through the crack, she didn't see anyone.

God, I'm losing it. How would someone have gotten in here? No one knows I'm here. I'm safe.

She had to work through seeing her ex-husband once more and the fact he had wanted to kill her family. Pushing into the room, she scanned it and sighed. "Fuck."

"If I wasn't on your side, you'd be dead by now."

The deep, decadent voice danced along her skin and she hated the way her belly flopped then flipped in response.

Masters stood behind her.

"Perhaps," she acknowledged, "but you'd also be dead." She pivoted and moved the Walther that had been pointing at him, letting him know she'd not been all that surprised he'd come up from behind. "I suppose I should be glad you're not in my bed."

"No, were I in your bed, you'd damn sure be glad. But that's not what I'm here about. I want an explanation."

Chapter Two

Masters fought the urge to strangle her. Anabelle Lee stood before him, with a weapon he'd not even seen trained on him.

It's the same one she held on me in my own bedroom. It took every ounce of his self-control not to touch her in a way that would shatter their working relationship into tiny little pieces. His libido and desire for this woman said it didn't matter, kill the damn working relationship anyway.

He noticed how she didn't toss the gun to the side but kept it in her hand as she walked back to the main room. He followed, doing his damnedest to convince himself he wasn't attracted to that ass in her jeans.

She sat and picked up her knife and fork, the Walther just within reach of her left hand. As he neared, she methodically cut the omelet into ten even-sized pieces. Her hair, wet and shiny, hung forward over her right shoulder and he wanted nothing more than to wrap those wet strands around his hand, yank her head back and…

He cleared his throat and claimed the seat opposite so he could watch her. He, on most days, was not a man who liked his back to the door, right now, it was fine. Anabelle Lee may be a lot of things but she wasn't about to let someone come through the door and shoot him. The only other option would be to claim the one beside her so neither of their backs were to the door. However, that presented its own challenges since he wanted to kiss her. Fuck her. Make love to her.

Nope, best to stay over here.

"And I'm still waiting."

She put a piece on her fork and lifted it to her full, lush mouth. "I'm eating."

"And I'm waiting. I'm not kidding, Anabelle Lee. What the fuck were you thinking?"

She chewed and swallowed before she opened her mouth again. "I was thinking of saving my family. I was thinking of making sure Ethan didn't lose his princess once more. I *wasn't* thinking of how this would affect you and make you upset for whatever reason."

"Let me see if I have this right." *Deep breaths. Breath slow and talk calmly. She's more volatile than you are, so if I lose it, we'll just be in the middle of a yelling match. Something that won't be productive in any sense of the matter.* "The three of you went to Africa to, what, kidnap Rally from her palace? Create an international incident?"

"One, you need to check your tone. Two, I didn't go with them. Ethan and I haven't exactly been chatty with each other since he found out Carlos was not just an ex-boyfriend but my ex-husband."

Don't blame him. I wanted to turn you over my knee for keeping that from me. Another slow, measured breath. And, for the sake of all that was holy, he began counting as well to maintain his control. *One. Two. Three.*

"I can understand his anger." *I have enough of my own.* "Why did you think you needed to go? And why didn't you come to me about it?"

Deep down, that bothered him the most out of the entire situation, because he believed they understood they could *always* come to him. *Did I get that wrong?* He'd been to each of their houses for meals, knew their Grams, or Mrs. Maybelle as locals called her.

"Why would I have? This wasn't a Theta Corps issue. This is family issue and we deal with that ourselves."

"Bullshit," he snapped. "Have I not protected you the best I could? All of you?"

She'd finished the fourth bite of her omelet and placed her fork down. She sipped some cranberry juice before she angled her head to the side.

"Again, you need to watch the fucking attitude. You're not my boss right now."

Words you don't need to say to me, Anabelle Lee, or I'm going to fuck you until we don't know what day it is. Holding on to the fact I am your boss is the only thing keeping me on this side of the table.

"This is me, answering your question. If you want to argue about it, come back later. I still need a few days to recuperate."

Fresh anger slammed into him at the thought of what she'd gone through. Of that bastard putting his hands on her, and not just in anger.

"Continue."

She licked the droplets from her lip as she nodded. "When I found out where they'd gone, I made plans to head over there."

"So you didn't know Carlos was there?"

"Not a fucking clue. When he stepped out of the shadows was the first time I'd seen him since we got divorced." Her entire expression tightened. "He had a gun on Rally. I volunteered to go in her place. That way, Ethan wouldn't be worried about her."

"What about you?"

She shrugged and ate some of the hash browns on her plate before frowning. Anabelle Lee added more salt and ketchup before another test bite and a nod of what he presumed to be approval. "What about me? I have been trained to deal with situations like this, not Rally. So, quite honestly, I didn't care. Had to protect my family."

"And when you two were gone from everyone else?"

"He took me somewhere in the back of a vehicle that had blacked-out windows. No clue where, because unfortunately I was still in shock about him being there and involved with this. I wasn't as focused as I should have been."

Her lip curled as she spoke and she shook her head. He understood how pissed and disgusted at herself she was. And he didn't harp on that.

"He bragged about a few things then began telling me what he was going to do to me once we reached our destination."

Masters flexed a fist. "And?"

She held his gaze with those damnable blue eyes and he hated how flat they were. He knew the answer before she even said it.

"I killed him the first chance I got."

That's my girl.

"How'd you get back here from Africa?"

"He'd drugged me and flew me back. We landed in Florida."

Masters thought about it. "You said you killed him but he brought you back here to the States. Where is his body?"

She shrugged. "No clue."

"I'm not saying you need to give me all details, Anabelle Lee, but if his body turns up at some point, we need to be ready."

She ate another bite, still no emotion in her gaze. "It won't."

"What won't?"

"His body. It won't turn up."

"Bodies don't just disappear. There's always a chance…"

She shook her head.

"He won't. Trust me."

"And the bleeding and bruises?"

"Complements of my time with him. I came here to recuperate and sleep. If I went home, my family would be there. When you leave, you can tell them you heard from me and I'm fine."

He crossed his arms and rocked back in the chair. "You seem to be mistaken on who works for who."

She sketched an eyebrow. "Am I?"

The chair legs hit the floor with a thump. He put his forearms on the tabletop and held her gaze. "Yes."

"If that's what you need to tell yourself." She finished her breakfast and drained the rest of her juice. "You know where the door is, so show yourself out. I have some sleep to claim before I leave."

He snapped his stare back to hers. "Leave where?"

"I'm going to Jamaica, if you must know. Rest and relaxation. Find me a nice, hot pool boy to keep me company."

"No, you're not." He almost laughed at the shocked expression on her face but somehow contained it.

"And you believe you have the right to tell me this why?"

"Because despite you seeming to forget I am your boss, I am. And I'm sending you to Russia."

She blinked a few times. "Russia? Why do I want to go there? It's winter." Her tone was incredulous.

"We have a job over there."

"Who am I working with? Ethan or Beau?"

"Me." The word slipped out before he thought better of it. That one eyebrow of hers jumped again, reaching for her hair.

"I'm sorry?"

He dropped his gaze to her lips then retreated to her eyes. "You heard me. You. Me. A room in Russia. And snow."

"You sure you want to do that?"

No. No he wasn't, not at all. But his mouth had gotten him into it and now he was stuck. "Scared, Anabelle Lee?"

"Of what? I know you won't do anything to me. You're not man enough to follow your emotions. You prefer to remain seen as the cold, uncaring boss." She leaned closer to him. "Let me know when you're going to wake up and take what you truly want."

She walked away and he groaned, scrubbing a hand over his face. "I'm so fucked."

For some reason, he'd wanted to get her alone, so he'd put himself on the op. Having her there wasn't a lie. He wanted her there. Flawless in Russian and with a good number of contacts, Anabelle Lee was a perfect choice for this op. Now he just had to find a way to survive being with her for so long without any supervision.

* * * *

Kirovsk, Russia

Falling flurries met Anabelle Lee as she stepped from the idling taxi that had brought her to this city above the Arctic Circle from the train station. Most of the trip had been accomplished on the rails, a way she loved to travel. He'd dropped her off right outside her hotel. The green color stood out against the snowy ground and there were Russian flags flying on the side of the building.

The winds blew, ruffling the fur on the collar of her white parka. Her pants and boots were also white. Her red hair had been braided and hung forward over her right shoulder, providing the only splash of color.

Jamaica would have been such a better place for me to go. Sun, sand, hot cabana boys she could have her way with and leave wanting more. She'd not been to this city for a while, but not much had changed. While she wasn't happy to be here, at least she wasn't out humping it through some terrain, reaggravating her healing injuries. This was an intel gathering op.

A job most times she wanted no part of, but Carlos had done a number on her. The burns on the insides of her thighs were proving to be the slowest parts to heal. She headed for the hotel to check in.

It was easy to get lost in mining cities, which was what she had hoped would happen. She needed to blend in and find out information. And on off time, she could go get in some skiing. A brief smile cracked her lips.

Fuck, that hurt. I need more damn lip balm.

She'd flown in to Murmansk and had hopped a rail down. The ride had taken more than a day so she'd spent time sleeping and making sure her weapons were set. She'd always loved train rides and cruising through the Russian countryside in winter on the rails was a sight to behold. Beauty was everywhere.

Her driver handed her the bag and, with a smile, she gave him a tip along with the fare then headed inside, anxious to get out of the cold. Gazing about the hotel, she made note of the people hanging around as well as the layout. She ambled to the reception counter and placed her bag at her feet. There were many clocks on the wall behind the counter, alerting people to times in other countries.

"I'm here to check in, please," she stated in flawless Russian. She didn't recognize the woman there and even if she had, there wouldn't have been any need for her to say anything. After all, she'd made a name for herself in this area.

It didn't take her long and she was heading across the polished white tile floor toward the elevator. She had a few freebies to utilize — Wi-Fi, a ride to and from the chairlift at the ski resort and breakfast. *It can work.*

Inside the room, she spun in a slow circle, taking it all in, and was more than happy to see a glass shower with robes hanging. *Nice and spacious.* A flat screen on the wall and two king beds. *Yes, this was going to work.* Since her contact here knew her as an extremely wealthy woman who dealt with things not so legal, it wasn't any shock for her to be using one of the most expensive suites in the hotel. At least until her place was ready for her to reside in once more.

She'd just gotten settled in when the familiar chime of her phone went off. She walked to the window to scan outside, then headed for the bathroom where she turned on the shower, all before she even contemplated answering the call.

"Hello?"

"I can't believe you didn't tell us about Carlos, much less that you were fine after he took you away from us at gunpoint. We had to hear it from Masters. Masters?"

"Hi, Ethan. Look, I'm sorry, we'll talk when I get home. Right now I'm busy."

"Where are you?"

"I'm not sure why you ask that question. I bet my money you have my location pinpointed on your computer."

"True, perhaps I should ask why the fuck are you in Russia instead of at home?"

"Need directions on how to handle your princess?" she queried, unable to hide the sneer in her tone.

It wasn't that she didn't like Rally — she just didn't feel the woman, a princess, was the right choice for her brother. Sure, she'd been a prisoner as he had. Sure, she appeared to be down-to-earth. But, damn it, Ethan was *her* brother and she didn't want to lose him to some woman who could hurt him and may not fit in with the family.

"No. Answer me."

"I told you I was busy. If I'm in Russia and busy, I'm sure you can figure out I'm working. I'm fine. I told you that. I'm here with Masters. I will let you know when I'm back Stateside."

She ended the call before he could say anything else. Right now wasn't the time for her to focus on her brother and his being upset with her for doing what she'd done. She wasn't about to apologize for it, nor would she lie and say she wouldn't do the same thing again if the situation happened once more.

Moving with stealth, she headed to her bag and pulled out a pen, while behind her the shower still ran in the bathroom. Uncapping the pen, she proceeded to use the item, which had a bug detector inside.

Sure, it wasn't the Cold War, but she wasn't an idiot and always checked rooms she stayed in. Anabelle Lee ensured she remained silent as she swept the entire room.

Clean.

She put it away and turned off the shower. After unpacking her few items, she settled down in the chair when a firm knock came to the door. She pushed to her feet and made her way there, doing her best not to grab for a weapon.

Get a grip, Anabelle Lee. This isn't going to be Carlos on the other side. The bastard is dead.

She peeked out and couldn't help the smile that kicked up her lips. Masters. He knocked again and she crossed her arms, leaning against the wall.

I wonder if he'll break in if I don't open the door for him.

Part of her wanted to see him do that, but she didn't. With a sigh, she ran a hand down the front of her white shirt before opening.

"Can I help you?" Her question fell from her lips in Russian.

"I brought those papers you requested, ma'am." He held out a packet.

Anabelle Lee stepped back and swept her gaze over him as he moved by her. Even dressed in khakis, a button down, and with black rimmed glasses, there wasn't any possible way to disguise the danger that Masters embodied.

She pivoted as he passed, closing the door behind her. A tendril of heat spiraled up from her gut, similar to a vine unfurling in the sun, at the sight of his firm ass in those pants. She was used to seeing him in jeans — which was a delight all its own — so the khakis were a change.

One I whole-heartedly approve of.

"Clear?"

His deep voice smacked her from her daydream of exploring that hard body beneath the geeky attire. Thoughts scrambling, she figured out what he meant. "Yes."

She approached the chairs and table he'd made himself comfortable at. Still, he didn't sit until after she did.

"What did you bring me?" she asked. "What papers? And by the way, you're looking smokin' in those khakis. You geek well."

Masters blinked a few times and she swore heat surged into his eyes.

"Blank ones." He tossed the packet at her. "What's your plan?"

While she hated that he was pushing the issue of work, they were there to do a job. She reclined in the chair, ignoring the manila envelope between them. "So attire is not a topic we can discuss. I put in a call to my contact when I was up in Murmansk but haven't heard back as of yet."

"You were there over a day ago."

"Really? Well, damn, guess that's why I was on a train for over twenty-four hours." She teased the end of her braid as she watched the man across from her.

Hard. Dangerous. Those were the first two words that came to mind when thinking of him. *Assuming I'm only being PG, of course. Otherwise it's sex and more sex.* Masters was one of those men others males were jealous of — fit and he wore the hell out of whatever he had on. It wasn't fair to the rest of mankind. Yet he never acted as if he gave the slightest damn as to how people saw him.

He was a man consumed by the job and he was damn good at it. That was part of the reason she worked for him and had first agreed to come to Theta Corps. The other was her insane attraction to him.

"Anabelle Lee?"

Is it fair to bring a woman to orgasm by just your voice alone? She didn't think so, but this man had the potential do pull it off. He had a voice the devil made to get women's panties to melt away. *Lord help the female population if he decided to use it as a weapon.*

Of course, he could just snap his fingers at me and I'd hand mine over.

He snapped his fingers and she started.

"What?" *I don't care what I just said, my panties are staying put. At least for the moment.*

"When will he be in contact with you?" Masters had a small furrow between his eyes and he frowned in her general direction.

"I never said it was a he. I said I had a contact and if I knew exactly when it would happen, I wouldn't be waiting, either." She fought off a yawn. "Now, if you'll excuse me, I'm going to slip into bed."

There wasn't any mistaking the heat flash in his eyes there.

She strode to the doorway separating her bedroom from the rest of the suite and with one hand on the frame, peered back at him. "Masters?"

He gazed at her, staring over the rims of his useless glasses. "What?"

"It's a king-sized bed, you're more than welcome to join me."

He flexed his fist but didn't move aside from looking back to the tabletop.

She chuckled and dipped into the bedroom. "You know, if you want to find out if I'm a true redhead or not." She left those words hanging in the air as she crawled between the coverings. She heard his curses and she smiled. She hadn't mentioned that there was another bed beside hers.

* * * *

"She keeps on like that and I'm going to jack off right here or go in the room and fuck her until I can get the need for her out of my system."

Masters stood by the window overlooking the city. His costume glasses were on the table away from him. He didn't need them. His vision was perfect. But it sold the image better.

He pinched the bridge of his nose and tried not to think of the woman sleeping in the other room. Seeing her dressed in all white as he'd come into the suite had been a punch to the gut, taking all his air.

This woman just didn't understand what it was she did to him. Then again, given her parting words, perhaps she did.

If only she knew how much I want to take her up on that offer.

But he didn't mix business with pleasure. Never had. Didn't have any plans on breaking that now. It served him well as head of Theta Corps.

Below him, in the cold snowy afternoon, people scurried about, like ants going and coming to their colony. People didn't talk to each other and avoided eye contact.

Sad state, but their issues weren't his. He had a job to do. Two, actually. Complete the mission and keep his hands off Anabelle Lee.

"No! Don't, please, stop." Her cry had him moving before he even contemplated the wisdom of bursting into her room unannounced.

Weapon drawn, he shoved through the door and scanned the space. It was empty except for the woman caught in the throes of a nightmare on the bed. Hurrying to the side of the bed she was in, he paused to make sure he to leave his weapon on a table and not where she would wake and see it in his hand.

"Anabelle Lee."

Masters called her name three times to no avail. She wasn't responding to his voice. Her cries were getting louder. Each second, he cursed her ex-husband even more, as the pure pain and fear in her tone ripped into his gut with jagged claws. He was going to have to touch her.

As the realization zipped through his mind, she brought forth her left hand, complete with the Walther she had under the pillow and swung it in erratic patterns, babbling and shouting.

No choice. She could injure herself, him, or discharge her weapon in the hotel, which would lead to an entire line of questions he didn't want to have to answer. Waiting until the sidearm was pointing in a direction that wasn't his, he grabbed her wrists and pinned them to the bed.

If she'd been crazy before, it was nothing compared to the wildcat who exploded onto the scene now. She bucked, kicked, bit and fought as if she were to die should she lose. Masters overpowered her and had her contained, unmovable, beneath him.

"Wake up, Anabelle Lee." Every ounce of his authority poured in his command.

He knew the second she had returned to him. Her blue eyes stared at him, clear and the confusion fading with every passing tick. His cock stirred when she flicked her tongue over her lips and cleared her throat.

"And here I thought you weren't taking me up on my offer."

God, the way that southern drawl of hers skated over his skin should have been a form of torture. Of course, she wouldn't address her nightmare.

She tried to move her arms, but he refused to let her. He had them pinned to her side but kept his focus on her face.

He gave a small shake of his head. "Release the Walther."

Those baby blues narrowed a fraction. "Why would I do that?"

"Because I don't want you shooting me for being on top of you."

"Were you that bad? I'm still clothed, so I'm guessing you lost your nerve."

One day, he was going to take her up on her dare. But not today, not after her nightmare.

"Release the Walther," he repeated.

"Or?"

Her breathing slowed and her pulse calmed a bit. He understood that that was her way of coping.

"I stay right here."

A ghost of a smile flitted along her mouth. "Maybe I like having you on top of me. How about you lose your clothes and I lose mine? Let's see if you can make me drop the weapon."

His cock thickened in his khakis. Her lids lowered and her gaze became shuttered. There wasn't any way she'd not noticed him hardening.

"Why don't you tell me about the nightmare."

"Filling in for the company shrink, Masters? What are your qualifications?" The biting edge had returned to her tone.

He increased his hold on the wrist attached to the hand with the Walther. When she relaxed her fingers, he plucked it from her and got off her lush body. Damn, he would have no problem spending hours exploring all of her.

Instead of moving away from her and the bed, he sat beside her, crossing his legs. "My qualifications are you're mine."

Her eyebrow jacked up quick as lightning.

"I mean you're on my team. I know my members." Cracking his neck, he waited a few more beats then handed her back the weapon. "And your screams are what brought me in here. So talk to me, Anabelle Lee."

"Threatening to pull me if I don't?"

"So much snark. No, I'm not pulling you. Believe it or not, Annie, I care."

She had been in the process of sitting up only to freeze and stare at him.

"What?"

She worried her lower lip and finished sitting. "Why did you call me that?"

"Anabelle Lee is your name."

With sure, steady moves, she began taking the braid from her hair. "You called me Annie."

Shit. I didn't mean to do that. This is what happens when I spend all this time around her.

"Who's Annie?" Her question had a chill to it.

Jealousy? From Anabelle Lee?

He stared at her hair as she raked her fingers through the thick, smooth strands, combing out the wave left from the braid. *Vibrant red. Such heat. Such passion. Just like the woman it is attached to.*

"You."

"No, I mean, who were you thinking about when you called me Annie?"

"I think of you as Annie." Masters couldn't come up with a single reason he'd shared that with her. *Aside that she asked you a question? Well, yes, there's that.*

"Why?"

Nope, I am not going there. "Tell me about your nightmare." Time for him to steer this back in the direction he wanted the storyline to go.

Up went the protective walls around her. "Nothing to tell."

"Nightmares aren't a sign of weakness. They are memories."

"I don't want these *memories*, if it's all the same to you."

"Had I known about them, I wouldn't have brought you here. You're not one-hundred percent and may be a liability."

"So get someone else then."

He shook his head. "I can't. It's too late for that, you know this."

"Me at less than one-hundred percent is still better than most of who you can find for this at their best." She crossed her arms with a huff of defiance.

"Perhaps, but I like people at the top of their game around me, not ones who are too goddamn scared to face their nightmares and try to work through them."

"You are such a fucking ass."

"I'm a boss."

"Sitting on my bed with me wearing nothing more than a shirt and a pair of panties. Want to know what kind they are?"

He bolted up and she laughed as she watched.

"Come on, Masters," she said, her drawl thicker and slower. Waggling her fingers at him, ever so slowly, she grinned. "Don't you want to know if I wear thongs or boy shorts? If I'm clean shaven or just trimmed?"

More than I will ever admit.

"No. I'll leave you alone to sleep if you're not going to talk to me about your nightmare."

She lay back and flashed some leg as she readjusted, sending another wave of heat to his groin. "Bye. But if you change your mind, I'll be right here."

He swore as he headed back to the sitting area, his cock hard and damn uncomfortable in his pants.

One day.

However, if this kept up, one day wouldn't be good enough with the vixen behind him, stretched out in that large bed, partially naked. She was driving him to the edge of any sanity or control.

Chapter Three

Music played in the background, ice clinked in glasses and women wore bunny ears on their heads as their only accessory to hot pink and black corsets. The panties were black, as were their shoes, but their stockings were some shade of pink she wasn't sure about. However, given the state of most inhabitants here, she didn't believe that mattered to them at all.

Annabelle Lee was no longer staying at the hotel, having hired people to open up her large mansion outside the city. It played to her coming back — it wouldn't have made sense for her to pay to stay at a hotel given she had lodgings less than twenty miles away. So she'd moved back in there and had come here tonight to meet her contact.

She twined her fingers around the stem of her coupe as she stared at the orange peel garnish within the drink.

Somewhere in this darkened building, Masters was watching her back. Anabelle Lee touched her side braid and shifted on the seat subtly. It wouldn't do for her contact to think she was nervous. Lifting her drink, she then enjoyed some.

"Ms. Ana."

Angling her head to the right, she gave a short nod when she spied her contact standing there.

"Yuliy, it is good to see you again." She put down her drink and extended her hand to the man standing there.

He took her fingers, bowed over them and brushed his lips along the back of her hand.

"And you. I was surprised to hear you were coming back here. You said you never wanted to return last time you left."

"Luckily, when one has as many investments as I do, I've got the ability to change my mind."

"Of course. My apologies."

She awarded him a slight smile.

"And I apologize for this, but there is a new player in town and once he heard you were here, he asked for an introduction."

"Heard I was in town?"

He stepped closer. "Hard for you to not be recognized when you arrive. Of course they were surprised about the taxi."

"And who asks for an introduction?"

Yuliy shifted uncomfortably, hands wringing an imaginary hat.

"Someone demanded."

"Yes, I am sorry."

With the bored sigh of a woman who believed this entire fiasco beneath her, she made a waving motion with her hand. "Bring him up."

"Thank you, Ms. Ana."

He headed off and she returned her attention to the groping men, gyrating women and all the other things she was more than happy to avoid on a daily basis.

During her wait, she thought about Masters calling her Annie. It was unlike him. Hell, it was personal. *Does he see more in me? Is this even the right time to try to figure it out? Probably not.*

She finished her drink and had waved for another when she noticed Yuliy returning, a man walking behind him, trying to appear more important than he was. The expression on Yuliy's face chilled her blood.

She actually liked this informant. He had a hard life and did what he did to make extra money to take care of his family. He'd never betrayed her and hadn't ever asked questions to make her think he could be playing another side.

"Ms. Ana," he said, waiting a respectable distance away.

"Come, Yuliy. Who is this you bring to see me?"

The man stepped past Yuliy and pushed him back. Anabelle Lee recognized his kind in an instant. The type who thought his looks got him a pass on being an ass. She couldn't deny that he was attractive, but his eyes, aptly called the windows to the soul, were serpentine.

"I'm Karvic." He ran his blue gaze over her body, a leer crossing his face.

Anabelle Lee didn't respond to his perusal of her figure. She had worn this dress for a reason. The pucker center, front and back, highlighted her form to perfection. The short to long flared hemline accentuated her baby-smooth legs and the strappy back showed off more skin to entice and distract men. She knew she looked hot. The hunter green of the dress complemented her red hair and tan skin.

The waitress appeared out of nowhere to replace her drink then vanished again. Anabelle Lee lifted the coupe and sipped once. "You say that like it should mean something to me."

He drew back but recovered quickly.

"No, I don't think you should know me, but you will."

"Are you worthy of this attitude you are trying to portray? Or is it nothing more than youthful posturing?"

"I've earned it."

Not short on confidence, this one. She inspected her nails. "I'm sorry, am I supposed to guess how you earned it, or are you going to stop preening and tell me?"

"I run a gang here in the city. We are one of the two tops."

"I don't deal in petty drugs." She waved him away as if he were nothing more than an annoying insect.

"If I could finish," Karvic said.

Yuliy stepped back and appeared as if he wished the floor would open up and swallow him whole. She didn't blame him.

Rising from her seat, she watched Karvic's eyes run over her once more. "Don't get it twisted, Karvic," she purred in a low voice, one he had to lean in closer to hear. "I didn't get to my position by letting little snots who run dime and nickel bags of shit around the streets to get in my face like that." She stepped to him until she had the ability to touch him if she wished. "Don't let the clothing fool you. I am not averse to getting my hands dirty."

He refused to meet her gaze. "I'm sorry, Ms. Ana. I spoke out of turn. I only meant to convey that because of my position, I would be available to give you prime information and intel if you were looking for any of that."

Karvic was a bit too eager and it set off all her flags to be cautious. Still, there was always a chance he meant every word he said and was acting squirrelly because of her and the clothes she wore. *Not exactly a good trait for a leader, but hey, it happens.*

"You bring me something and I'll see." She walked past them both and left without so much as a farewell.

After a final stop in another club, one she also frequented, Anabelle Lee made it back to her home. She dropped the green and gold clutch on the settee as she strode with single-minded determinedness to the drink bar.

She'd finished her first bit of vodka when the door opened, admitting Masters.

"Well?"

"Always so impatient," she chided, fixing him a drink. "What are you doing here? Came to see if I needed help unzipping?"

She faced him, a mocking smile turning up her lips.

"We both know you saw the back of this dress and there aren't any zippers there, but go ahead. Take a look and see if you know how to get me out of this thing."

He flexed his right hand, but didn't approach her.

"What did you learn?"

With a careless shrug, she sashayed toward him, offering him a vodka she'd just poured when he'd entered. Their fingertips brushed and she damn near dropped the glass, the spike of electricity there too much to handle.

Anabelle Lee filled him in on Karvic and the offer he'd brought to her. As she spoke, she made her way to the master bedroom, where she stripped out of the dress and put on some silk pajamas.

"So do you have a key to this house, or are you breaking in?" She reentered the room and found him by the window, looking as imposing as ever.

"I have a key."

"And if I have a man in here with me, should I put a rubber band on the door handle so you know and don't interrupt us?"

While she had the chance to see his features, there wasn't any way she missed the tensing of his entire body. For whatever reason, picking on him was getting more and more gratifying. Yes, it was childish, she couldn't deny that, but watching him struggle to retain the iron hold on his control was such a dare to her.

Could she break it?

Could she make it snap like a twig?

Would she finally be able to get him to face her and see her as a woman and not someone who worked for him?

Just like they said in school, the ones who pick on you are the ones who like you the most.

"You're not here to get laid, Anabelle Lee. You're here to do a job."

"I'm well-aware. Not my first rodeo, you know."

She refilled her drink then carried it and a packet that had been left for her over to the couch and sank on it, curling her legs beneath her.

Masters spun and she gazed at him.

"What's that?"

"I asked for some information on the groups I used to be in bed with. I haven't been Ms. Ana Volkov for a while now. And I wanted to make sure I didn't go back and make a mistake."

He grunted his approval and claimed a seat across from her. "How can I help?"

"You can't. No offense, but this is an intel gathering mission and you know how those go. I just need a refresher on my stuff, all my holdings, so I don't get tripped up. Nothing else to be done. If you need to sleep, go ahead and use the bed. I'll be out here for a few hours." There were plenty of other rooms in this house but she'd only asked for one to be prepared for the time being. Tomorrow a few more would be opened and aired out.

She wasn't flirting with him. Her mind had clicked over to work only and that was where her focus had to stay until it was over. There had been many missions where operatives took shifts and shared the one bed they had. This would be no different.

Except he's not your brother or cousin and you don't want to jump them with every heartbeat as you do Masters.

Right, should be a walk in the park.

Not.

Masters did not argue with her. He just strode to the king-sized bed and stood beside it, staring at the pristine white covers. All he could see was the spread of her red hair along the surface, clashing with the purity of the coverlet.

He ripped off his shirt then sat on the edge to unlace his boots.

"Did I see the dress? Of course I saw the fucking dress. It looked as if it had been painted on her," he grumbled to himself and the empty room.

He'd wanted to punch the person with her in the face for looking at her. Hell, the entire club population had watched her as if she were about to be their feast. Yet, none had treated her with disrespect — in fact, it had been more fear he's seen when they'd looked at her.

She'd been here undercover for over two years and he had no doubt her reputation still carried over from those days. He'd read the reports and knew some of what she'd had to go through to survive and maintain her spot at the top. However, like with all operations, there were some snippets of information that hadn't made it into the file. He had no doubt that was what had happened in her case.

Placing his boots off to the side, he closed his eyes and rubbed the back of his neck. Exhaustion hit him. He'd been going nonstop for a long time now and needed a vacation. This wasn't it, but at least he could grab some sleep and not worry about someone coming into the room to kill him.

Unless he'd done something to piss off his redheaded fighter.

Standing, he undid the button on his jeans, slid them down over his hips and laid them across a chair with his shirt. Back at the bed, he drew the covers down and slid between the sheets, sucking in a sharp breath at the cold.

It didn't take long, however, before he was warm. Shifting to his side, he slid a hand beneath the pillow and drew it back quick. Reaching over to turn on the light beside him, he moved the pillow and saw a Beretta there. He checked under the other three pillows on the bed and found she had a weapon under each one.

"Ahh, Annie, what a world of mistrust you live in."

Yes, he was in the same world, but he only had one gun beneath his pillow in his bed. He was able to leave it at work.

Except when I got the news she had been taken.

He pushed that memory away and clicked off the light. Sleep found him moments later. He woke to his phone vibrating against his leg where he'd left the item.

"Masters."

"Sorry to bother you, boss, but there's been an incident involving Kevin McNeal." His secretary, Mino, was on the other end.

He jolted up in bed and reached for his clothes the second the light was on. "Talk to me."

Kevin had come through the ranks with him in Theta Corps and headed his own team. They were friends, despite Masters having poached one of his best agents from him not too long ago. Bailey Hyde — well, now she was Bailey Vinokourov. One of the best assassins he'd ever had the pleasure of meeting and not through a scope.

"All we know is his car went off the road. He's not in a good way and all signs point to sabotage — his brake lines were punctured."

"So they've ruled out accidental puncture?"

Phone between shoulder and cheek, he shoved into his pants.

"Correct. Too many holes of the exact size, all made by the same item." A door clicked shut. "They don't think he's going to make it and I know you're in Russia, but he's been asking for you."

"Give me a second." He put down the phone and tugged on his shirt. He picked up the phone once more and he continued, "Let me talk to Anabelle Lee and I'll get back to you."

He ignored his boots and hurried down the hall to the living room to find Anabelle Lee reading in the same place he'd left her a few hours earlier. A fire burned in the hearth and she had some old-school R&B playing low in the room. She was singing along with Gladys Knight.

"And I appreciate that," he said, remarking on the lyrics she sang.

She jumped and swore as she faced him. "Damn you. I thought you were sleeping."

"I was. Mino called."

"What's up?" She put all her attention on him and not the papers in her hand.

"McNeal has been in an accident and is asking for me. They don't think he will make it."

"Go. This is nothing more than recon and intel gathering. I'll be fine."

"You need backup. You didn't exactly have friends when you did this before."

"A person in my position isn't going to have friends. I'm cold and ruthless." She reached for her cup of tea and took a sip.

"Yeah, you look it."

Angling her head, she gave him a Cheshire cat grin.

"What do you think makes me so damn good at my job? Do you want me to call a cab for you?"

"I've not decided if I'm going yet."

She snorted. "You need to go. McNeal is your friend and I'm guessing that's a particular pool which is limited in its swimmers."

Truer words have never been spoken.

"You sure you'll be okay?"

"Fine." She waved a hand. "Go."

Dialing Mino back, he hadn't even said hi when she began, "I'll have the car pick you up at the airport. I've got you booked on the first flight out."

"Thank you, Mino. How are things there?"

"Fine. Beau's not peed on anything inside for at least two days so we're all real proud of him for that."

From her tone, he had no doubt the man in question was right there, hearing her words.

"Give him a cookie."

She snickered. "Will do. See you after you get here, sir." She was gone.

"A car will be here for you in about ten minutes. They'll take you directly to the airport."

He shoved his phone in his pocket and stared at the woman lounging on her couch, wearing nothing more than a black satin gown and matching robe. Her hair, which she'd gathered in haphazard fashion on the top of her head, showing off her swanlike neck.

Her beauty hurt his eyes. And she wasn't flirting with him. No, quite the opposite. She was working. Hell, she'd not even looked at him as she'd delivered the information about the car coming to pick him up and take him to his flight.

"Anabelle Lee."

She flipped another page and only then did she look over at him. "Yes?"

"Be careful."

"I always am." She went back to work on perusing the sheets before her.

Despite her bravado, he saw the shadows in the depths of that cobalt-blue gaze. He admired her more than he'd ever share with her. The way she was able to put her own fears aside to get the job done. Yes, it was part of the life they had chosen, but it didn't lessen his admiration. Never would.

"I'll be back as soon as I can."

She waved him on without looking at him. Masters ground his jaw but headed for the door. Seconds before he yanked it open, she called out to him.

"Maybe you can find that zipper when you get back."

He smiled and walked out to the waiting car. All he needed now was McNeal to hold on until he got there. Regardless, the farther the car took him from the woman he'd left, he was already counting down until they were going to be together again. Him and Anabelle Lee.

Chapter Four

The smell of bacon, eggs and more filtered down to her nose, tempting and coaxing her from deep sleep. With a hand wrapped around her Walther, she slid from the comfortable bed and headed up the hall.

Peering around the corner, she smiled as she saw the man cooking the food.

"Grams would be pissed if you showed up at the breakfast table packing heat, cuz."

Beauregard stood there, clad only in a pair of blue jeans that hung low on his waist. Dark hair touched his shoulders and she skimmed over the present scars on his back. Her cousin had been in some scrapes, no joke.

"She'd be more pissed if I allowed myself to be killed without defending myself from an intruder."

"I'm making you breakfast. What kind of killer does that?"

"You."

He glanced over his shoulder and winked. "But I'm family."

"Exactly why I think the way I do." She lowered her weapon and walked farther into the kitchen. "What are you doing here?"

"I finished an op early and came here when I heard about McNeal."

"Any news?"

"Nope, but it doesn't look good. Bailey and Masters are there with him."

She didn't need to think about Masters. "I'm going to change."

"Better hurry. This bacon is almost done and I'm splitting what's left when you come back, not what's there now."

A warning she took to heart. Tugging her turtleneck down over the waist of her black jeans, she made her way to where her cousin waited with her food.

"Damn, that was fast. You need to teach other women how to get ready quick."

She rolled her eyes and went for the plates. "You should up the quality of women you fuck."

"The women I pleasure are perfectly happy with the arrangements."

This time she snorted and about dropped the plates as she took them to the table. "Stop deluding yourself. You have several exes who I'm sure wouldn't have an issue killing you if they saw you again."

"Like yours?"

Cold slammed into her and she put her gaze on his waiting one. "Really?"

"You never told us you married the fucker and he did come back to kill you."

Point taken.

Beau carried over the food and distributed it on each plate. Then he grabbed the coffee and filled both mugs.

"Eat."

At the mention of her ex, her appetite had vanished. Still, she obeyed her cousin's order. It had always been that way—other than Grams, Beau had called the shots, given out the instructions and taken care of her and her brother. It didn't matter that she was a grown woman— if he wanted her to eat something, she would sit and eat.

Staring at the food before her, she saw he'd done her eggs how she liked them—over easy—crispy bacon and two pieces of wheat toast, both slathered with butter.

"Thank you."

"Why didn't you tell us?" he asked as he sipped some coffee.

"It wasn't important."

"Excuse me? Seriously? You married him, brought him into the family, you're goddamn right it's important."

His anger was palpable.

"Let it go, please."

"And he isn't coming back again, is he?"

"Not unless hell has an early release program." She bit into a piece of bacon.

A smile crossed his face, one which would scare those who didn't know him. Hell, even some who did should have been worried by that expression. "That's my girl."

The rest of breakfast was spent talking about Grams and people around home. She was glad it was this one who'd shown up as opposed to Ethan—he wouldn't have let it go that easily. He would have pressed on what she'd gone through and how she was recovering from that. With Beau, he didn't push. She must have passed the test.

She refused to say she was fine—there were still nightmares. A smile flickered over her lips as she thought of Masters being on top of her.

"Share."

She blinked and looked at her cousin. "Huh?"

"Whatever is making you smile that way?"

She shook her head. "No, thanks."

He scowled at her, but she brushed it off.

"You don't scare me, Beau. We're family."

"I'll tell Masters."

She ate a bit then glanced back to him. "Sure you want to do that? Not positive how good you are in with him right now given all the harassment you've been giving Mino. You know he loves her."

Beau harrumphed and dug back into his food.

"She starts it."

"Perhaps, but Masters is going to finish it. Christ, man, if you want her just ask her on a date. What's stopping you?"

Emerald-green eyes slammed into her. "What's stopping you?"

She leaned back and finished up her most current piece of bacon. "Well, for one, I don't swing that way so I have no need to take her for one. Two, Mino and I have gone out for meals together. I like her."

"I meant Masters."

Her stomach bypassed her feet as it sank below the marble floor. "Why would I ask him out?"

Beau reclined in his chair, tipping so the front feet were off the floor. "Let me let you in on a secret, little cuz. You would have been better off instantly denying it like you do most things that it's just an honest no for. How long you been interested in the boss man? And does he know about it? Have you slept with him? Is that what was going on over here?"

She held up her hands, wanting to end his tirade before he got ramped up. "Let me stop you right there. I don't have a thing for him. I'm not interested in him. No, I haven't slept with him, and fuck you for thinking that's what I'd be doing on an op. I'm not you, Beau. I can keep my pants closed, along with my legs."

His smile grew bigger.

"Is that a fact?" he drawled.

"Fact." She curved her hand around the coffee mug and wished for a moment he was a mute. Or not here. But the breakfast was wonderful and so that almost made up for it. Almost.

"Here are some facts for you, Anabelle Lee. I've known you since you were in diapers, hell, I changed some of them. I've seen you with all kinds of guys and there is one thing that you had in common with all the ones you liked. When you think or talk about them, you squint your left eye. Just a bit, but I notice it."

She drew back. "Liar."

"That what you want to go with?" He rocked forward and got to his feet. "Come with me."

She followed him to a mirror in her front room. He positioned her before him.

"Who's our boss?"

"Masters." *Fuck.* She saw it the moment she said his name. A miniscule change, but leave it to her eagle-eyed cousin to pick up on it.

"Any more excuses and lies you want to get off your chest before we continue this conversation?"

"I don't even want to continue this conversation, so we can let it drop and I'll be just fine with that."

"Life's full of disappointments. Get used to it." He guided her back to the table where their breakfast remnants remained. "So what's the story between the two of you? Do I have to kill him?"

"There's not any story, Beau. Let it go. We pick on each other. That's it. There's a line we don't cross." She pursed her lips. "Like you and Mino."

He narrowed his gaze and she pushed back from the table once more.

"Anabelle Lee," he warned.

"I have to get to the club. I think it's time for a surprise spot inspection. I'll be back. If you're coming with me, you need to put on a suit. I don't have men working for me who can't dress like they don't have more than two pennies to rub together. Put your hair back in a ponytail or one of those damn manbuns and clean up."

Thirty minutes later, she met him at the door and nodded at his attire. He looked her over and groaned.

"I'm going to be killing guys for trying to get into your pants. What the fuck are you wearing?"

She looked down at herself. "It's a banded jumpsuit. What? I wear tight clothes and show off my assets. It's what I do."

"It's a damn good thing Grams isn't seeing you in that. Let's go." He held the door for her.

She reached for her white fur coat and slid it on. The outfit had racerback tank stripes, a zipper down the back and side torso cutouts. There wasn't much left to the imagination for sure. Finished off with a pair of fitted pant legs of the same color and her boots. Also navy blue, like the clothing, were her lace-up ankle booties with a heel of five and three-quarters combined with a hidden platform. She loved them and had missed them.

Rubbing her cheek on the fur, she waited for Beau to take her arm and escort her to the waiting Land Rover. He held the door and she slipped into the back seat.

"I also wonder what Masters does when he sees you in attire like this."

So did she, but she wasn't allowing herself to think about him right now. She immersed herself in the role of Ana Volkov as Beau drove. All the while, though, she did wonder how her cousin had gotten there, since there weren't more car tracks.

Knowing him, he parachuted in then humped it through the night. Or if that wasn't enough of a challenge, he would have parachuted onto the roof and let himself in one of the windows up there.

As he parked in front of the club, she eliminated thoughts of everything but the job at hand, including Masters.

* * * *

Masters stood immobile beside Bailey. Her husband, Ivan, was on her other side, arm around her waist, supporting her. Silence filled the room as they said their final farewells to his friend and the man who she had known as an uncle for most of her life.

They were the only three left, as everyone else had departed. Masters wasn't going to leave until she did. Slicing his gaze to the left, he watched her. Nothing. Her face was a blank slate. No tears, no emotion. No anything.

"Bailey," he began.

"Not now, please, Masters. We hadn't necessarily made up after everything, but he was still loved by me."

"He never doubted your love, not once."

She shifted and Ivan lowered his head to kiss her temple. "I'll leave you two alone to talk for a bit. I'll be in the back if you need me." He spoke Russian then slipped away without another sound.

Masters moved his line of sight from Bailey to the framed photo of McNeal. An old service picture. He looked regal and handsome.

"If you require some time off," he began, only to close his mouth when she shook her head.

"No, I'd just assume work. So if something comes up and you need me, send for me." She raked a hand through her short, spiked hair and rolled her shoulders before moving to the side and claiming a seat.

"I will." He took a chair beside her, stretching his legs and hooking his ankles.

Silence between them, they passed the time, lost in their thoughts until Ivan walked back in and stopped beside his wife. From his peripheral vision, Masters witnessed the tenderness in Ivan's expression as he cupped Bailey's cheek.

He averted his eyes while getting to his feet. "I have to get going. If you need anything, Bailey, let me know."

She met his gaze. "I want the fucker who did this. You find out who and send me."

He thought for a moment, not wanting to approve those heading for personal vendettas, but damn if he didn't want a piece of the fucker, as well.

"I'll keep you informed, Ivan."

With a brief nod, he strode from the church and into the waiting vehicle. After a short drive, he climbed into the jet and closed his eyes as they began taxiing down the runway. He would get some sleep now. He'd been up since he'd gotten the news about his friend.

* * * *

The front door slammed and he listened to the consistent tapping of her heels on the marble floor. His body shifted from waiting to ready — and not for a fight, but for passion, sex and everything else that he experienced when he got the chance to look upon Anabelle Lee.

For a few moments there wasn't anything, then in a blink of an eye she stood in the doorway to the living room. Her brilliant-red hair snagged his attention, as usual.

"You okay?"

He remained on the sofa, slouched back, a drink dangling from his fingers.

"Been better. How's the surveillance going?"

"As it should. How's Bailey?" She tugged on the fingers of her black leather gloves one at a time until they'd been removed.

He paused, yanking his attention from her movements. *Damn, even that is sexy when she does it.* "She's a hard one to read. I don't know her as well. I would guess hurting, but she wants the man who did it."

Anabelle Lee removed her coat next, leaving her in a tight gold dress that stopped mid-thigh, hugging her curves. He gulped and tightened his hold on the glass.

Holy fuck, she's hot. Fuck if he didn't want to lower the zipper, tooth by tooth, exposing her creamy skin to his gaze and touch.

She threw the coat to the back of a nearby chair, not even looking in its direction, just lobbing it with an easy toss. "Didn't think you had conclusive evidence what happened to McNeal was intentional yet. Has that changed?"

"No." He lifted the tumbler and took a solid drink of the amber liquid. "She doesn't care. Bailey, however, feels he was murdered."

"She's got good instincts. If she feels that, she may be right." Anabelle Lee made her way to the bar and fixed herself a drink.

Masters ogled her ass in the gold sequin dress, wishing he were drunk enough to not know better and go to her, yank up that material and bend her over bar. It was so painted on her body, he doubted she even had panties on.

Easier access.

"How well do you know her?"

Anabelle Lee downed her drink in one gulp then yanked on the shoulder strap and shrugged. "Not as well as I'd like. I met her a few times when we were searching for Ethan. But it's not like we have a standing date for dinner. I know her sheet and I figure she's even better than that if you brought her to your team."

"Why is that?"

She gave him a quick look before creating another drink for herself and taking a long, slow sip before she answered. "Because you, Masters, hate failure. You want the best around you."

"Is that so?"

"Of course. That's why I'm here." She flicked her wrist and drained the rest of her drink. "I'll be back."

More of that temptation in heels and gold sashayed her ass away from him. He swore a few times and finished his drink as well, while she was in another room. When she returned there was no longer a dress covering her figure. No, this time it was workout pants and a black oversized sweatshirt with the Georgia Tech logo on the front. She'd thrown her hair up in a ponytail and had fuzzy on socks.

The difference stunned him and yet either look made him hard as stone and wanting to fuck her. He groaned and shifted on the seat. She vanished into the kitchen and came back a few minutes later carrying what he guessed to be a mug of tea. Instead of sitting across from him, she claimed the other side of the sofa he was on and tucked her legs beneath her.

"You never answered my question. Are you okay?"

"I did. I said I've been better." *How the hell does she smell like that? Moonlight and roses. I fucking swear I've never come across anyone who smells as sinfully delicious as this woman.*

"Look, you come after us and make us talk in situations like this. He was your friend."

Masters looked at her, unused to this side of her. "I'm the boss. I'm allowed to ask that kind of questions."

Anabelle Lee shrugged and took a sip of her tea before licking her lips. "I'm a woman."

He cocked an eyebrow and gave a slight shake of his head. "I'm not following. What the fuck does that have to do with anything?"

"Not a goddamn thing. Precisely the same as you stating you're the boss — it means shit. Despite it all, everything we do, the fights, the sniping, we're friends. I'm here if you want to talk to me."

Not quite what I want to talk to her about. His had less verbal and more tactile or physical communication.

Although he wasn't averse to hearing his name fall from her lips in a breathless tone.

"Ready to tell me about what happened between you and Carlos and the nightmares you've been having?"

Her gaze shuttered and he figured he'd gotten to her. "Sure."

Had he been standing, a breeze would have been able to take him out. He'd not imagined she'd agree. Not in a million years. Anabelle Lee was the second most private person he knew, her cousin Beau being the first. Not that Ethan was a chatterbox, but the man appeared as one next to her.

"Sure?" he echoed.

"Yes."

Well, fuck.

"I was kidding, Anabelle Lee, you don't have to do this."

She sipped her tea and watched him with those unblinking cobalt-blue eyes. They weren't judgmental or anything similar. "Carlos is the cause of my nightmares," she said in a soft tone, breaking the silence, her drawl so thick he almost didn't understand her.

Her fingers held the mug so tight, he saw the color leech out from them.

"When I saw him again, all the old memories came flooding back. But the second he threatened to kill my family, I agreed to go with him, just to get his guns off the boys."

He set his glass on the end table and angled toward her, eyes fixated her.

"Ethan and Beau had seen his psychotic mindset before me. I was too enamored with the idea of being in love," she admitted, an overwhelming amount of self-loathing apparent in her voice. "The more they tried to warn me away from him, the more I hung on because I was determined to prove them wrong. I should have listened. Their pushing eventually had me marrying him. I'm not saying it was their fault—I'm the one who married the bastard—but it was all to show my independence."

Her gaze glossed over and he couldn't tell what she was looking at anymore, him or the memories she spoke of.

"I found out what he was truly like when I came home early one day. Early as in a few days early, not an hour or so. The house was silent, so I thought he was at work." She shuddered and took a moment to center herself.

Masters had to force himself to remain in his seat and not move closer to her, just to put his arms around her and offer some strength. The agony in her words ripped him apart as if someone had torn into him with razor-sharp claws.

"I guess I was partially correct. He was working, just not what I had expected him to be doing."

He had a feeling he would regret asking his next question. "What was he doing?"

"He was cutting into women while he fucked them. The bedroom had been covered in plastic and he was"—she gulped—"digging little sharp points into them as he screwed them. They couldn't talk, because they had no tongues. Other men watched and some were fucking each other as he took the women." She shook her head. "I didn't confront him. I snuck away and called the cops."

It was shame he heard this time. Bile churned in his gut—this was all new to him.

"You said 'them'. There was more than one in the room?"

"Yes. I counted four women lying there, tied spread-eagle so they were there waiting for him whenever he wanted them. I don't know who they were or how he got them there. Like I said, I left and called the cops."

"Then what happened?"

"I don't know. This was right when you hired me. I had come home early to tell him I was leaving for my first mission in Iran. Your final words to me were not to do anything to get noticed by the cops, don't do anything stupid. I don't know how he got away, probably has a contact in the police. I waited until I saw the cars arriving before I left. The papers never mentioned him by name."

"It wasn't your fault, Anabelle Lee." *It is mine because of the words I told you. If you'd not killed that bastard, I would hunt him down and gut him like a motherfucking fish.*

She snorted. "Sure, it was. I should have killed him then."

"Did you have enough to take them all out?"

"Doubtful, but he would have been dead."

"And you could be, too." Not an idea he found appealing at all.

One shoulder rose and fell. "*He* would be dead."

Masters wanted to go to her and pull her close, but he remained where he was. "And? How does that help your family? Or any of your friends and those who love you?"

"My actions would have kept him from hurting others. You know he told me he increased the number of women he went after to hurt. Said just because he could, he wanted to do it. As a punishment for me calling the cops and leaving him."

"How did he find out it was you?"

"Like I said before, I think he had someone in the police department. Or a few people. I don't know." She put down her mug and withdrew her hands until only the very tips of her fingers peeked out from the material of her sweatshirt.

This was the first time since he'd met her that Masters had seen Anabelle Lee appear vulnerable. The blank look, the shivers that rolled over her, the hitching breaths and more.

Masters got up and moved nearer to her until, when he again sat, his thigh touched part of her leg.

"What happened after you left with him?"

Anabelle Lee drew a small circle on her knee before her fingers vanished once more. "He beat me, cut me, burned me. Raped me." She had no inflection in her tone.

Masters clenched a fist and wished the fucker was here right now, because he longed kill him all over again. "How did you escape?"

"I told you, he brought me back to the States."

He wasn't going to let her shut down, not now that, for the first time in their relationship, she was opening up to him like this. "No, that's not an answer. How did you get away from him?"

"Why is that so damn important?" she snapped, drawing back.

"Because you need to remember how fucking good you are. You must to find that part of yourself this fucker still owns, you *need* to find it and squash it beneath the heel of your stiletto shoe or your goddamn cowboy boots. I don't care which you use, it only needs to be done. There's something you should remember. *You* got away, *you* survived and *you* killed the bastard."

He kept his tone hard as he tried to get her to see how he viewed her.

"But I let him hurt me. I let him take me." A slight wobble appeared in her tone.

He ignored it. That wouldn't help her, pointing out that he saw her vulnerability. "You did what you thought best to keep your family safe. There is absolutely *no* harm or shame in that, Anabelle Lee."

"Sure, there is. I was messed up before but now I'm totally screwed in the head."

"No, you're not."

"Tell me something then, Confucius, what guy wants a woman who can kill him in numerous ways and who has nightmares at night, which may inadvertently have me killing them, anyway, even if I don't mean it?"

He refused to focus on her with another man. "My advice would be to stay away from the boys and find a man."

"You sound like Ethan and Beau. And where should I look for this man who is going to ignore my faults?"

She asked—Anabelle Lee was the one who opened the door. Masters didn't think further on it, just reacted. They weren't faults. They were things that had made her into who she was, who she had become. He didn't have any other thing to do but one final option—lean in and kiss her.

Chapter Five

Anabelle Lee held immobile with Masters' lips on hers. Warm, firm and better than she'd believed a kiss had the potential to be. He began to move away and she snapped her arms out and gripped the back of his head as she angled hers and opened her mouth. She needed this, what he could provide, even if it was just for the moment. That was how she lived, moment to moment. She never hoped for anything more than a moment in time.

Slipping her tongue into his mouth, she moaned as his was there to meet and tangle with hers. He yanked her over onto his lap with a deep growl, fisted his hands in her hair and plundered her mouth. She shifted so her knees were on either side of his hips, bringing her core in close contact with his groin.

All the hair on her body stood as if she were out in the middle of an electrical storm. Energy pulsed through her, bringing her back to life. She tugged on his soft hair that streamed through her fingers and kept her mouth mashed against his. Wriggling on his lap, she purred at the feel of his thick erection between her legs.

Words vanished. They weren't needed. He shoved his hands up the back of her sweatshirt, sprawling along her spine before moving to the front and cupping her breasts. A low moan slipped free and her breasts grew heavy with want.

He teased her nipples and plucked at them, making them ache for more. She squirmed again on his lap. He tore his mouth from hers then ripped off her sweatshirt, after which she pulled on his shirt and it soon followed.

Masters cradled his hands along her spine as he bent her backward, giving him free access to her breasts. She cried out and begged as he sucked on them, until she panted with need. When he allowed her back up, she kissed him again, thrusting her tongue deep, as her hands went to work on the snap of his jeans. After the zipper was down, he lifted his hips and helped her tug them enough to free his cock.

While she did that, she'd also stood and kicked off her pants before climbing back on the man seated before her. Forehead to forehead, both breathing hard, she curled her fingers around his cock.

"I've waited far too long for this," she muttered, beginning to stroke him. Anabelle Lee wanted him and had for a long time. In those dark places at night, this was the man she thought about, dreamed about, wished to have with her.

His answer was to put his hand between her thighs, shove aside her panties and tweak her clit.

"Fuck," she cried out with a tremor.

Her body clamored for more but he kept a slow, antagonizing pace of torment while she pumped her hand along his shaft. He had one hand on her ass and the other bringing more wetness to her slit as she grew impatient for his dick inside her.

"Please." The word tore from her mouth as he slipped one thick finger up inside her.

She rocked hard against the digit and he grunted then added another finger. Her teeth chattered as she tried to keep the scream contained. Just when she believed she'd done it, he flicked his tongue over her sensitive nipple once more and the scream volleyed from her throat.

He covered her hand with his own and rubbed his cock between her pussy lips. She held her breath and waited. It wasn't long before he pushed into her with a continuous stroke. With his cock embedded inside her, he moved his hands back to her hair and gripped two handfuls. Putting their gazes together, he held that stare.

Masters rolled them so she lay beneath him, the smooth leather of the couch cold beneath her skin, but she didn't care. The heat spreading through her because of the man above her would banish any chill.

He fucked her.

No other word for it.

Thrusts that moved her along the couch until she couldn't go farther had her crying aloud. During the entire thing, he never once let go of her hair. He forced the eye contact and she didn't have a way to break it. Not that she would have, if she'd managed to find a way.

Masters fucked her through three back-bending, mind-blowing orgasms before he began to slow. She held on to him, sweat running down their bodies. The air around them filled with the scent of sex. She didn't mind.

All of it was what she'd needed. By the time he found his release, she'd lost her voice and couldn't scream anymore.

Wrapping around him as tight as possible, she closed her eyes, leaving him deep inside her and his large body atop hers. She was warm, exhausted and, most importantly, she felt safe.

Anabelle Lee woke with a start only to calm. It took her a moment to realize what was going on. Masters had moved them to her bed and she lay enclosed in his embrace, her legs wedged between his.

"Go back to sleep," he said without moving.

I didn't make a sound. How did he know I was awake? It could just have easily been a twitch in my sleep. "When did you bring us in here?"

"About two hours ago. Sleep."

The fact it hadn't woken her spoke volumes of how safe she felt with him, to sleep through being picked up and moved. She opened her eyes to darkness. Turning her head, she heard his heartbeat and his nipple brushed along her cheek. Desire stirred inside her once more.

"What time is it?"

"Christ, Annie, just go back to sleep." His voice was deep and raspy, because Masters had that low sexy voice.

Warmth exploded within her at that variation of her name. She liked it. From his lips only.

Instead of listening to him, she moved her head and flicked her tongue along his nipple then drew it into her mouth, continuing to tease it with her tongue.

"Fuck," he muttered.

"That's my intention," she admitted, moving one hand down to grasp his thickening erection. She curved her fingers around him and began stroking.

He bucked his hips, driving his dick farther into her seeking touch.

"Good," she whispered. She pushed him until he lay on his back. She dipper her head and kissed him. "It's my turn."

Alternating between kisses and swipes of her tongue, she made her way down his chest until his cock was right by her mouth. She smelled his earthy male scent. Stroking his shaft, she readjusted to a more comfortable position and licked up the length.

"Yes," he drew out, fingers delving into her hair.

"Yes?"

"Come on, take me in your mouth. Suck my fucking cock hard until I hit the back of your throat and come."

She needed no further encouragement. Running her tongue along the rim of the head, she the blew on the tip prior to licking the top. The taste of his pre-cum had her opening again and taking him in deep.

"Yes, oh, fuck yes, just like that. Deeper. Take it all. Come on, Annie. Take it all."

His words and his hand on the back of her head were with her as she deep-throated him. Bobbing up and down on his length, she used her free hand to play with his balls.

Masters didn't ask, he just dragged her leg over so she straddled his chest, facing his dick. She never stopped sucking until he pulled her back and she felt the first puff of his breath along her pussy.

He captured her clit and sucked hard as he fucked her with three of his thick fingers. She trembled and ground back, pushing more onto his face. He took it, even as he began pumping his hips, driving his dick farther into her mouth. She didn't typically enjoy sixty-nining with a man. *Hell, this, I can't get enough of.*

They both came at the same time. Thick ropes of cum shot from his cock and she didn't stop until he had nothing left to give. He stopped eating her and slid her hips down until they were over him. She rose up and sank down on him, eyes fluttering once more as he filled her.

Her moan turned to a squeal when he sat up, lifted her with ease and flopped her face-first on the mattress before he took her from behind.

* * * *

Masters stood in the shower, hands braced on the marble tile lining the large stall. The hot water streamed down his body, fogging up the glass so he couldn't even see out into the rest of the master bath. Not that he wanted to. He was okay with berating himself in private. Anabelle Lee lay sleeping in her king-size bed where he'd left her. For one whole day all they did, sleep, eat and fuck. She'd told him earlier that Yuliy would be calling her with a time and a place, but until then she just had to wait.

To be fair, he had no problem with spending that time in bed with her and allowing her some much-needed sleep. Now, however, he was away from the temptation and was more than free to yell and condemn himself for messing with a woman in a position beneath him.

She was beneath me for sure. And above me. Beside me.

Christ, his memories were going to kill him. It wasn't what he had intended on doing, but once he'd crossed that line with the first step, there hadn't been any going back for him.

He turned off the water and opened the glass door. Steam billowed out and, when it settled, he saw Anabelle Lee standing there, dressed, holding a towel for him.

"What are you doing in here?" he demanded, taking the towel and wrapping it around his waist, willing his cock not to tent it.

"Figured I would come see if you were raking your ass over the coals for what happened between us. From the look of discomfort on your face, I assume you've been doing just that." She shook her head. "Let me set your mind at ease. I know what I did, so you being in a position of power didn't sway me to do this. I went into that completely willing."

His cock disobeyed him when she ran her hungry blue gaze over him. She dropped her stare and licked her glossed lips before meeting his eyes once more.

"So willingly." She cleared her throat. "Anyway. You're off the hook of the self-thrashing. No need to go to those lengths."

"We can't do this again." Even as the words passed his lips, he wanted to take them back and say they should do it again, like right this mother-fucking instant.

"Agreed."

What the fuck? She agreed without needing to think on it at all? *She can't pretend she didn't enjoy what we did, so why is she so fucking anxious to pretend it didn't happen and agree it won't, or shouldn't, happen again?*

He swallowed his disappointment and frustration and walked to the mirror. By the time he swiped his hand over the fogged-up glass, she was no longer in the room with him.

Once he'd shaved and dried off, he pulled on a black mock turtleneck and tucked it into the dark blue jeans. Then he padded from the room and sat at the edge of the bed where he'd just had the most explosive night of his life. One he wasn't allowed to repeat.

There were times he hated his job and how it kept him alone. This would be one of those. He tied on his heavy boots and got to his feet.

Walking to the living room and kitchen area, he was met by the scent of breakfast cooking. He gazed into the kitchen and saw Anabelle Lee standing there over a skillet, flipping whatever sat in there.

He cleared his throat and she didn't look in his direction, just gestured off to the right. Turning his head, he saw a plate full of pancakes, eggs and bacon sitting there.

"For me?"

"You've been to each of our houses and know damn well that if we cook we feed those there. So, yes, for you. Christ, are you going to make this all kinds of weird now, Masters?"

He tore his gaze from the food and back to her. She had one hand propped on a shapely hip and there was annoyance stamped all over her features. He wanted her back to normal and this was it. Sarcastic and snarky.

"Wouldn't dream of it," he commented.

"Good, because there's no reason to make anything of it. We were two consenting adults. End of story." She focused back on the food in the skillet. Her own pancakes. "Eat."

Plate in hand, he strode to the table and sat. She had put coffee and juice out for them both, as well. He fixed his coffee the way he preferred it then added syrup and butter to his pancakes.

They ate in silence. Were he eating with any other woman he would believe she was pissed at him and was expecting him to purchase something for her. Not with Anabelle Lee—she just didn't talk while eating.

He cleaned up with her then called Mino while Anabelle Lee went to shower and get dressed for the day.

"Hey, boss."

"Mino. I need you to pull all you can on a man named Yuliy Markov."

"Anything else?"

"Yes." He went to the window and placed a hand on the glass, needing the chill to help cool him down. "I need you to dig up more about Carlos."

Mino paused. "You mean the one who Anabelle Lee killed?"

"Yes, give me all his contacts and anything out there. And find what's not. I want to know what that fucker ate for lunch in kindergarten."

"You do know he's dead, right?"

He ground his jaw. "I'm perfectly aware, Mino. Why are you questioning me?"

"Because I've already pulled up everything on him when you first asked me to do that. Just curious as to why you're looking for more information on a man who is no longer of this earth."

Masters heard the tap of Anabelle Lee's heels on the marble as she neared.

"Don't ask, Mino, just get it done. I want it on my desk when I get back." There was something else about that man Anabelle Lee had not shared with him and he wanted it all. Yes, he'd checked it before, but this was different. He needed another look.

"So, you're coming home soon?"

"Yes."

He turned in time to see her walk into view. Anabelle Lee instantly owned any room she entered. His blood dropped to his cock, thickening and lengthening it. A halter top in dark metallic gold had a deep V-neck that allowed him to see the sides of her boobs. And if that weren't enough, the sexy top she'd taken and combined with a black floor-length skirt boasting two side slits. He was simultaneously blessed and tortured by a flash of toned leg with each step she took.

Her red hair fell free around her shoulders, giving her even a more tousled and damn sexy look.

"Fuck," he uttered.

"Boss?"

Damn it, I forgot Mino is still on the phone. "Never mind, just get it done, Mino."

"Sure thing."

She hung up and he shoved his phone back into his pocket with a muttered curse.

"How's your girl?"

He snapped his gaze to Anabelle Lee. "Excuse me?"

"I assumed that was Mino on the phone with you. You don't call anyone more than her." She grinned. "Plus, you called her by her name." She chuckled as she spun to the left, giving him a perfect view of the open back.

"Something happening this morning I don't know about?"

"Why do you ask?" She poured herself some scotch.

"Because it's nine in the morning and you're dressed like you're going out to a club for dancing and drinking."

She faced him, a sarcastic smile on her face. "Don't worry, Dad, I'll be safe." Anabelle Lee took a drink, set it down then plumped her breasts, all without dropping his gaze. "Not my first rodeo."

He had to bite back his growl of fury. *I'm the one who told her it was a mistake. I have no say over this. Besides, she's doing her job.* A job she knew and took very seriously.

"You letting me in on it?"

"Nope. You told me I was here to gather intel. That's what I'm doing. I am not handing over my contacts for you." She messed with her hair a bit then drank the rest of her scotch. "I'll be in touch."

Not in the way he wanted, but he would have to learn to forget how it was being with her. *Not until I'm dead and buried. Hell, maybe not even then.*

"Everything lined up?"

"Yes." She hiked one of the slits and he groaned as the black matte of a .22 strapped to her upper thigh flashed to his hungry gaze. She readjusted the Velcro before tugging the skirt back over it. "I understand we don't work together all that often, but I'm good. I know what I'm doing."

"I know you do." *Just like I am positive I want to be that gun on your leg.* "But you're going in without backup. I have to check."

"You do what you have to." She plucked her black fur coat from the back of a couch and slid it on, hiding her form from his ogling stare. "I'm heading off. It's been real, boss, see you back in the States."

With a toss of her head, she walked out of the door, the tap of her heels fading the farther she got.

Masters hated this. He wanted to be in there with her, just in case. But that was not how this worked. She had her part to play and he had his. She was going to pick up the intel and send it along to Theta Corps so they could work on removing this most recent threat.

He didn't need to be seen as following her around, so he was leaving today ahead of her. According to Mino, Anabelle Lee had a flight the next day so she would be home soon after him.

It didn't take him long to get his things ready to go and he was sliding into the back of the taxi he'd requested. The driver barely looked at him, just drove him to the train station where Masters waited two hours for his train.

Have I said how little I like this? No? Not in the last five goddamn minutes, so let me say it again. I don't like it. At all. I should have stayed with her and made sure everything went smoothly. She's got no fucking backup there.

His unease stayed with him during his trip home and he had no doubt it wouldn't leave until he laid eyes on Anabelle Lee once more.

Chapter Six

"What the hell do you mean, Mino?" Anabelle Lee wanted nothing more than to get home and take a long hot shower.

"I'm just the messenger, don't take it out on me. He wants you on that plane and off to Chile."

Anger spiked, Anabelle Lee kept it contained. It wasn't Mino's fault her boss was being a pussy. She didn't deserve getting her ass chewed by a pissed-off Anabelle Lee.

"Fine. Did you expect me to go with tight dresses from Russia? I could but I like some of those outfits." *Especially the fit they gave Masters.*

"Of course not," she said. "I got your green go bag from your closet. It's on the plane waiting for you."

She scanned the grounds as if it would allow her to find Masters hiding around a corner or something like that. Nothing. Mino waited before her, a blue windbreaker hanging down to her knees. Behind her, a black Cadillac Escalade waited, idling. Warm.

"Go," Anabelle Lee ordered. "I'll get on the plane. I'm going to assume there is a dossier or two waiting for me."

"Everything you need to be caught up. For what it's worth, welcome home." Mino waved and jogged to the back of the vehicle and slipped inside.

"Right. Welcome home." The words fell from her lips, drenched in sarcasm. So instead of heading home where she would be welcomed by her shower, she was now heading to Chile.

At least it will be warm there. All I know is when I get back, Masters and I are having one hell of a talk.

She climbed into the G5 and claimed a seat while the door closed behind her. Immobile until they reached cruising altitude, she rose and made her way to the bar. Opening the cabinet, she sneered at what she found. Leaving it alone, she spun before going farther to the back and digging into some of Masters' private stash. She headed back up with a bottle of his Laphroaig Triple Wood firmly in hand. She opened it and poured herself a healthy amount before reclaiming seat to peruse the files waiting for her.

She read and slept on the flight and had showered, changed and been rejuvenated by the time she climbed off the plane at the small airport in Chile. A jeep drove up as she stood there and she smiled when her cousin's familiar John Deere cap came into view.

"Hello, gorgeous, can I give you a lift?" he asked, drawing to a halt beside her.

"It's been so long since I've been picked up along the side of the road, so yes." She batted her eyes. "I do so love to depend on the kindness of strangers." With an eyeroll, she tossed her bag in the back and vaulted up into the passenger seat. "Take me somewhere nice."

"Oh, you'll love it, darling. Dirt hut, wiping with a leaf, it'll be the time of your life."

She snorted and reached for a bottled water resting between them. Uncapping it, she sighed then took a long swig. "I think my contribution to the party will be a bit out of place."

"Aw, fuck, Anabelle Lee, did you rob his stash again?"

"Hey, it was on the plane I was on. I wanted a drink and it was there."

She always took from the stuff he put on for himself when Masters flew. It was fair in her mind. They were the ones out there sleeping under the open sky and risking their lives. Not him.

"One day, little cuz, you're going to push him too far."

Talk between them turned to the assignment as they careened along narrow roads. Her body began to hum with excitement. She loved her work and wouldn't change it for the world.

Her cousin hadn't lied. It was a hut and she groaned.

Beau glanced over to her. "Problem?"

"I came from sleeping in a king-size bed on satin sheets and now I have to sleep on dirt. All without my bed between them."

"Sucks to be you. I came here from my big-ass bed, but I've been on the dirt for a few nights now. Stop being a diva."

She didn't even waste her time flipping him off, well aware that was part of his goal, to get under her skin. "Why haven't you moved in?"

"Waiting on you."

"Aren't y'all always?"

He slammed the brakes, snapping her forward and spilling the water on her shirt.

"Asshole," she snapped, wiping it away best she could.

They climbed out and she reached for her bag then followed her cousin to the first hut. Along the walls were maps and weapons. She spied modern technology as well, but for the most part, it was hard to get readings through the thick foliage of the jungle, so while satellite photos were there they weren't as complete as local maps tended to be. Many of the trails seen were false ones.

Anabelle Lee dropped her bag and strapped on her weapons then strode to the small group gathered around the table in the middle of the hut. As they reviewed their information, she braided her hair.

Beau tossed her the stocking cap at his side and she tugged the olive-green wicking wear on. Hands resting on the butts of her side arms, she stared at what they were looking at.

"Game plan a capture, or has that changed?"

"We've not heard different, so we go with capture. This fuck we're hoping can help tie in something with The Watchers."

She nodded. "I read the file and I remember them. Where's Valentino?"

Beau crossed his arms. "He's got the kids. And Jaydee is off somewhere doing something so secret not even Masters knows. So Giovanni has their children."

She never looked away from the papers scattered on the table before her. "Did you ask Mino?"

Beau sketched a brow. "Why would I ask her?"

Anabelle Lee moved to his side and patted him on the shoulder. "Haven't you figured her out yet? She knows all that Masters does and more. She's all of our confidant. And she likes Jaydee. That woman could run Theta Corps if she wished."

Beau grunted. "I don't care, though. I'm not the one who asked."

She rolled her eyes. "True. Just food for thought in the future when you're trying to get Mino to find some information for you."

"She always tells me she's not helping me."

Anabelle Lee walked around the table and pointed at the map's edge closer to the side she was on now. "That's because you're a playboy, jerk, and an ass. I wouldn't help you, either, if I were her and you treated me how you do her. Where's this spot? Looks like a great place for an ambush. It's a bottleneck. We could secure him there, hopefully without any extra loss of life." She allowed her fingers to drift over the area she spoke about.

"No," one of the locals spoke up. "They are aware of that area and never go without sending through an advance team."

She shrugged and met his dark gaze, not at all perturbed by the sound of the defiance in his tone. "So what? We let the advance team move through untouched and unbothered. We can be quiet enough so they don't know we're there. Then when the target comes through, we take him."

"I'm with Anabelle Lee," Beau said. "We need to nab him where we have the most control of the surroundings. Plus, he doesn't know we're onto him. Unless there's a leak and someone informed him."

"My men are loyal, sir."

"See they stay that way," Anabelle Lee said. If she hurt someone's feelings, she didn't give a damn. This wasn't a hand-holding adventure—they were out to capture and potentially kill targets. She would do whatever was necessary to keep her group safe.

Beau kicked her under the table and she grunted. Okay, so it may not have been the best thing to say but, damn it, she was tired. So damn tired and wanting a vacation, not to be here sweating in the jungle about to get into yet another fire fight.

Not much later, they left the hut to vanish into the thick foliage. They moved in relative silence, not speaking, not joking. That night, after they stopped, they made a fire for protection against the animals roaming the darkness.

Anabelle Lee made her bed against a tree trunk, her automatic weapon laid across her lap. It didn't take her long to fall asleep—sleep was grabbed when available. That was a fact she'd learned as a rookie in this business. Some times there wasn't sleep for days, so when the chance was presented, operatives always took it.

Beau tapped her the moment she was up for watch and she went to the stump he'd been on and settled in for her time. Many people didn't like being on watch, but she didn't mind at all—it was her time to think, to run over the plan, make sure nothing had been missed.

She had everything ready by the time the others woke. That was what they endured for five days as they humped over the landscape to approach from the north. On the final day, she brought up the rear and kept an eye on those with them. Two men from the area and two others from Theta Corps.

They all took their positions and settled in to wait. *I hope to hell this man didn't change his route.* That night there was no fire—it couldn't be risked that their targets would smell the smoke in the area before they passed through.

She lay against a thick branch, feeling very serpentine as she waited for the advance party to get through the pass. Eye to the scope, she waited. So many people thought their jobs were always full of action, but the truth was that most of the time it was a waiting game. Wait to get to the location, wait for the target, wait for the exfil.

She didn't mind however — she loved this job. No one moved and she lined up for her shot when their target approached.

Anabelle Lee waited for Beau to make the first move — this was his op. His shot cracked the stillness and everything happened at once after that. The sounds of automatic gunfire exploded as the men with the target fired blind into the landscape around them, trying to protect the one they were supposed to protect.

Not going to happen, guys. She took them down one at a time as the three guys with her did what they did in eliminating threats and securing the man they were after. A man in dark clothing raised the muzzle and pointed at her cousin, or she thought it was a man.

Not seeing the person with it, she calculated as if they were crouched and with swift adjustments, dropped her weapon to hit them lower and fired. Once. Twice. Lowered the rifle again and shot twice more on the off chance they'd flattened themselves out when she'd first fired.

Back on the ground, she made eye contact with Beau, who sent her a nod. Grateful he was fine, she wiped the sweat and dirt off her cheek as she moved from body to body checking them to see what they could pull.

After walking into another small section, she froze. With a gasp, she looked back to where she knew she'd been lying in wait. This was her kill. A child lay there, not much more than ten.

"You okay?" Beau called out.

Hell no, I just killed a child. "Fine." Bile rose in her throat and she gulped it back before reaching out to close his eyelids. "Rest in peace," she murmured. Standing straight, she walked away saying a prayer for him.

They headed for their exfil and Beau was beside her. The two others had control of the prisoner.

"What's up?" he asked.

"Nothing."

"What the fuck happened back there, Anabelle Lee?" His tone had turned to the overprotective older cousin in a heartbeat.

She wasn't going to talk about it. "Nothing. We did our job." The nausea returned and she reached for her water, took a small sip and held it in her mouth to rinse it out.

"Beau," Hamilton called for him.

"This isn't done," Beau said to her prior to jogging off to meet Hamilton.

"Yes, it is," she vowed. *Another nightmare to add to my ever-growing list.* She sent the stream of water down to the ground before swiping her hand across the back of her mouth.

She kept to herself more so than usual as they returned with him to the States. She waited until after the debrief then strode down the hall to the office of the man she had to see. Although the time neared midnight, she had no doubt he was still there.

Entering without knocking, she strode up to the desk. Masters looked at her as he put his pencil down.

"Knocking is a practice many use, Anabelle Lee."

She sneered. "I don't give a fuck. Two things. You want me away because you can't handle the fact you slept with me, at least have the goddamn guts to tell me to my face instead of sending Mino to do your dirty work. Second, I'm on vacation."

He expression didn't move with her first statement but with the second one, his brow furrowed. "Excuse me?"

"I'm taking myself off the roster. From this moment on, I'm unavailable."

Masters narrowed those dark eyes of his. "What brought this on and until when?"

That boy's sightless eyes stared at her, reminding her once more that there were certain aspects of her job she didn't enjoy. "None of your business and until I come back and tell you my status has changed." She pivoted on her heels and strode for the door.

"Anabelle Lee."

She paused with her hand on the doorframe. "What?"

"I didn't agree to this. I have more things we need you for."

But not anything you, specifically, need me for. "I don't give a damn. Find someone else." She gazed back at him. "Either you give me the time off or I quit this damn company. Your choice. I don't give a rat's fuck, I'm leaving now. You decide and let me know."

She walked out and headed home.

* * * *

Masters stood at his desk waiting for Beau to show up. He stared over the city and sighed. He'd thought she was going to come back. He'd thought she was just blowing off steam, but she'd not answered calls from Theta Corps, nor had she returned to headquarters.

"You wanted to see me?"

"Come in and take a seat," he said without turning around. He watched the man's loose-limbed gait as he did as told in the reflection from the window.

"I have nothing to tell you about Anabelle Lee, if that's what this is about."

That got him to turn. Beau hadn't sat, instead he stood behind the chair, arms crossed and legs braced apart appearing the ever-confident and dangerous man he had the ability to be.

"Ethan told me you asked him yesterday about her."

Damn family. Can't keep a fricking secret with them.

"It is, but I have a different question for you. What the fuck happened in Chile?"

"Nothing other than what was in all our reports."

That wasn't right. She'd been through worse ops and hadn't walked away from Theta Corps. From him. Masters took his seat and leaned back in the leather chair.

"Something happened, Beau. You had to have noticed a difference in her behavior at some point."

"I know my cousin. I asked her, she said nothing was wrong. I took her at her word." He canted his head to the side. "Something you used to do."

"And you believe her now?"

"Fuck no. But she's not going to tell us anything. We had to send in the big guns."

Understanding sank in and Masters nodded. "Mrs. Maybelle."

"Grams asks and we answer." He shrugged. "Other than that, I don't know what to tell you, Masters. She's not taken a vacation before so maybe that's all it is. She needed some time off."

"She threatened to quit if I didn't give her the time off."

His brow rose. "Interesting, that I didn't know. Did you not want to give her the time off?"

"I need her here." *Where I can keep an eye on her and know what she's doing.*

"Why?"

Masters stared at Beau. That one word was lined in brotherly concern and a not-so-veiled warning.

"Because she's an asset to what we do here."

Anabelle Lee's cousin gripped the back of the chair he stood behind. "You have plenty of people who work here that are capable."

Masters thought on what to say. Beau was a hell of a lot smarter than most people gave him credit for upon first seeing him. Many thought he wasn't more than a dumb hillbilly, backwards hick, based on his slow southern drawl and the John Deere baseball cap, and they couldn't have ever been more wrong.

He had two doctorates, one in geothermal physics and the other in engineering. He may have more now. And if he wasn't careful, he would say something to alert this man Masters had slept with his cousin. That would be dangerous for him. Of the life-threatening kind of threat. Those boys protected Anabelle Lee without fail.

"Not like her."

"True, most of the people who work for you aren't as foul-mouthed as my cousin. Still not answering why you need her here. Most people take vacations from their jobs, Masters. She's not had one since starting here. If you told me no, I'd be pissed, as well. Give her the time off, let her work through whatever it is she needs to and move on from there."

Because I'm part of the problem, I have to make sure she's okay.

"Fine," he groused. "I'll stop by and have a chat with her."

"Good luck with that. I wouldn't go today."

"Why?"

Beau headed out of the room, only to stop at the entrance. "Because Grams is with her and, trust me, it's going to be enough of a pain for you to explain to myself and Ethan why you slept with her, but you sure as hell don't want to explain it to Grams." One final look of warning and the one-man army disappeared.

How the hell does he know about that? No way he could have. He was bluffing. However, now that he thought about it, Ethan wasn't as warm as he usually was — granted, none of the Jackson crew was over-the-top friendly, but there'd been a definite chill in his demeanor, as well.

He reclined in his chair and drummed his fingers on the desk.

"Masters."

He opened his eyes to find Mino entering. "Yes?"

"Paperwork for you to sign." She waved one hand full of sheets and in her other she held two sheets.

"And those?"

"Not sure if you'd made up your mind on Anabelle Lee. One is a leave chit granting her leave and the other is a termination paper."

"I'm not firing her," he snapped, irritated Mino would even think that.

"I know. It's actually the menu for the dinner you're attending Friday night. They faxed it over and wanted to make sure you were okay with everything." She put the stack down. "These are requisition papers for the ammunition and other weapons we need to replenish."

"Don't I have someone to do all this?" He glanced at her sideways. "Like you?"

She snatched the papers back and left the pen in his hand with nothing to write on. "Fine," she growled. "Just don't get pissed I am signing your name." She was out of his office in a few seconds.

He pinched the bridge of his nose. "I'm just not winning on any level here."

He pushed away from his desk and walked to hers. Mino was on the phone.

"Yes, he's fine with the menu, says everything appears perfect. Thank you so much for sending over a copy of it so he could take a final look. You have a wonderful day also." She laughed. "No, I'm not going to this, it's way above my paygrade. Bye, Shellie."

"Am I going to like the menu for the dinner with the top brass?"

"Should have looked at the damn menu." She slammed her drawer closed. "And I'm offended as hell you would ask me that. If you don't trust me by now, fire me, as well."

He didn't have time for this. Hands on her desk, he glared at her. She didn't back down. In fact, the fire in her eyes grew.

"What is going on with everyone around here? Do you need a vacation, as well?"

"I'd be more than happy to take one but you wouldn't be able to do your job without me." Her words were tight and sharp.

"Take a vacation then, Mino. I don't need you. Christ, what is going on with everyone?" He headed for the elevator. "Fill out your forms and take the time you need to get your head back on straight." He punched the button and waited for the car to arrive.

He stepped in and waited for it to transport him down to the basement and the gun range they had in the building. He needed to get rid of some stress. Only after he'd ruined fifteen targets did he calm down a bit and get more in control of his emotions. He returned to his office floor and stopped exiting the elevator when he didn't see Mino there.

Maybe she's on lunch break or something.

Striding to her desk, he noticed it was all clean as it was by the end of her day. Not liking the feeling of unease creeping up his spine, he entered his office. Nothing out of the ordinary, just how he left it, with one exception. A single sheet of white paper sat in front of his chair.

"So she went and took a vacation as well." His irritation grew once more.

Snatching it from the smooth surface, he stared at it. Three words stood out to him. *Tendering my resignation.*

He swore as he sank to his chair, unable to move by that statement. *Is she serious?* His heart thundered behind his ribs and he rubbed at the furrow between his eyes.

He yanked the handset off the base and called her phone. The ring was echoed by her desk. *Fuck!* He rose and went to her desk, pulled open the drawers until he got to the bottom one where the phone sat with a sheet of paper taped to it.

Theta Corps property.

The urge to roar in anger swarmed him. He took several deep breaths, shook his head and took a couple more. It didn't work, not even in the slightest way.

"Let me recap," he said to no one other than himself. "One of my best agents just put herself on a vacation for an undisclosed amount of time and now my secretary up and quits on me. I'm having the fucking greatest week."

He grabbed her phone from the drawer and pulled the contacts. She'd deleted anything personal from the device, leaving only Theta Corps contacts.

Masters stomped back to his office, kicking the door shut behind him. *My day has gone to shit and, look at that, it's not even noon.*

Chapter Seven

"You have to forgive yourself, Anabelle Lee."

She tucked some hair behind her ear and sighed. "Grams, I've tried. Don't you think I've tried to convince myself I'm forgiven?"

Anabelle Lee sat curled up on Grams' couch while she worked on a square for the quilt being created. Grams sat in her chair, sewing another square on. While Anabelle Lee hadn't any idea what this one looked like all spread out, she had no doubt it would be stunning.

"I don't think you've forgiven yourself if you have to convince yourself of that fact." She put down the quilt. "You've always been so hard on yourself. If you weren't as fast as the boys, couldn't do as many pull-ups, it didn't matter. You'd berate yourself for days."

"Not a great pep talk, Grams."

Mrs. Maybelle Jackson laughed, her blue eyes still vibrant and sharp. "This isn't a pep talk. This is you getting your butt kicked so you get out of this funk you've allowed yourself to fall into.

"Yes, ma'am."

"So do you want to tell me about what happened in the jungle?" She turned her square over, showing off the forest image it held.

"Not really."

"Very well. Hand me that square you were checking on."

Anabelle Lee passed it over and reached for another square. This one had magnolias on it and she smiled before she set it aside and went for another. She spent her afternoon with Grams, picking out squares from the immense collection gathered over the years.

Then they made dinner together — chicken-fried steak with white gravy, fresh biscuits, green beans, and macaroni and cheese.

"I have something for you in the garage before you leave, baby."

"What is it, Grams?" She dipped her finger in the gravy.

"Some of your things from a while ago that I've been holding on to. I think they may be better off with you in your place."

She wasn't sure what it was, but she didn't mind taking it off Gram's hands. "Okay."

After they ate and had chess pie for dessert, Anabelle Lee cleaned up. She felt better but had by no means healed from having taken the young boy's life. Accompanying Grams into the garage, she waited for her to point out what was for her to take.

"Right there," Grams stated.

"I'll get it." She moved a few boxes then withdrew the one she spoke of.

"What's in it?"

"Take it home and open it. Go on, I will see you later. Thank you for cleaning up."

Anabelle Lee exited the garage and headed for her vehicle after kissing Grams on the cheek. Box on the passenger seat, she fought off a yawn then drove home. Once she'd changed into some sleeping attire, she opened the box and smiled.

Her paints and brushes.

"Thanks, Grams."

Perched on the edge of the couch, she pulled out each item and lined them up on the dark brown coffee table before her. She had a lot of items in the box and, quite honestly, was surprised Grams hadn't thrown it away.

"Not even sure any of these paints are still good."

No time like the present to find out. In the bottom of the box were some small pieces of old canvas and she withdrew them with a sigh. Smoothing her hands along the material, she closed her eyes and inhaled deeply, allowing the scents to flow through her.

As she held the canvas to her face, wonderful memories swamped her. Painting out on the back porch while Grams quilted or worked in her garden. Doing projects for school and seeing the joy on Grams' face when she brought them back to her. Hell, she still had some of the later pieces she'd finished in the house she still used.

"Grams always was smarter than any of us. Perhaps she's right and I need to get back into painting."

It didn't take her long to cover a section with newspaper and spread out the canvas. She uncapped each of the paints and separated them into two groups — keep and toss.

Once she'd finished, she allowed herself to do a small painting. Nothing huge or extravagant. Just a small scene from her property toward the back where it met her siblings' property lines. A waterfall fell into a nice pool before dropping underground and feeding the lakes.

"Definitely not my best work, but it's a start."

Grabbing another canvas piece, she took her time to set up and eventually did another. Four hours later, she cleaned up and went to bed. The next morning when she woke, the second her eyes opened she knew there was someone else in her house.

Rolling from bed, Walther in hand, she snuck up the hall to find her brother sitting on the couch checking the paintings she'd completed yesterday.

"Put that away," he ordered. "You're not going to shoot me."

"Day just started," she quipped. "Who knows what's to come?"

Ethan glared at her with a shake of his head. "You've got a mean streak."

"What are you doing here, Ethan?" Anabelle Lee set the Walther on the bar and dipped into the kitchen to start some coffee.

"Can't a brother stop by to check on his baby sister?"

She narrowed her gaze. He was up to something, no doubt. "I'm your only sister. So, what gives?"

He smiled. "There is the fact that you're my only sister."

She tugged up the shoulder of her sleep shirt. "Not in the mood, Ethan. What's going on?"

"When are you coming back to work?"

Those blank brown eyes staring up at nothing flashed before her mind's eye and she shook her head. "No clue." *I don't know if I will come back at all.*

"Beau told me what happened."

"What does he think went on?" She forced herself to relax.

"Please, that Mensa motherfucker knows way more than we give his redneck ass credit for. So stop playing. He told me about the boy you had to take out to keep him safe."

Nausea began to churn once more and she gulped a few times. *How the fuck did he know about that? He never once went by the kid.*

"Not the first time it's happened and probably won't be the last." *Therein lies the problem. Children should at least have a chance at life.*

"So what's the problem? Why did you walk away from work?"

"Look, what right do you have to judge me? You don't know what I'm going through and no, I'm not going to tell you."

"You're breaking up the team."

She exhaled sharply and poured her coffee before adding the sugar and cream. "So I should come back to work because you don't want to work with anyone else?"

"We know how the other thinks. I'm going to have to learn someone else's quirks and get familiar with them."

Her spoon clinked against the side of the mug as she stirred. "Basically, you want me there so you don't have to break in a new partner?"

"That's not what I mean and you know it." He shouldered her aside and grabbed a mug of java.

"No, I don't. That's what you are stating. And I don't get it. You're the one who began breaking this up long before I did when you fell for your princess."

Ethan went still as death.

"Don't bring her into this, Anabelle Lee."

But she was angry and pushed. "Why not? You want me back at work after I put a bullet in a kid who wasn't much over ten if he was at all. But you being with your princess began the largest changes of all. You're not going on as much as you used to so I'm paired with Masters and others. I had to go with Beau right after Russia because you were with Rally and couldn't be bothered. Wait, how was it put, you were on a 'vacation'. Get off your fucking high horse. I could be on a well-deserved vacation. I've not taken one since I started working for Theta Corps. You have. Beau has. But I've not."

Ethan ground his jaw but didn't drop her gaze or look away.

"Which is it then, are you on a vacation or are you quitting?"

"Fuck you, Ethan. I've been home for one day. One. You know what, get out and go back to your perfect little princess."

"Anabelle Lee," he growled.

"No. No! I'm not doing this. Get. Out." Lord, she wanted to stomp her feet and point.

Ethan shook his head but stepped away from his freshly made coffee. "Just so you know, Rally likes you. I wish you two would get along."

She blinked but didn't say anything else. Ethan held up his hands then walked out. She didn't move until she heard the click of the door. Only then, did she allow herself to crumple to the floor, mind whirling with unending images of the child.

* * * *

"Mino!"

No response. Masters dropped his pen on his desk and shoved back to stomp to the door.

"Mino."

The desk was empty. As it had been for the past week.

"Damn it." He'd forgotten she'd given him her resignation. He'd hoped this was a phase, hoped it wouldn't have lasted. And she would have come back. He wasn't going to chase her down. Not her, and certainly not some goddamn redhead vixen who haunted his dreams.

Back at his desk, he pulled up a list of contacts from his address book, searching for the one he needed.

"I survived before she came, I'll do so again." The pep talk did shit to make him feel better. In fact, he went from bad to worse, especially when the name he wanted wasn't there.

He swiped the phone she'd left behind, checked there and sighed in relief as it popped up.

"May just take me a long while."

"Masters?"

"Come in, Beau. What do you need?"

He whistled low. "Damn, never realized how much Mino curbed your temper. Why don't you just ask her to come back and apologize for whatever you did?"

"What makes you think I did anything?"

Beau sketched an eyebrow.

Masters began typing the information into a new contact on his computer.

"You can transfer all of that at once, you know," Beau said, laughter in his tone.

"Is there something you needed?"

"Yes. I need you to get Mino back. You're a fucking bear on a good day, but she dulled your teeth."

"I'm sorry, are you the boss here?" He leaned back in his chair. *How the hell do I transfer this all at once?*

"I pulled the short straw to come talk to you about this. You have been worse than a honey badger with a toothache. Go talk to her." He walked out of the door. "Ethan can help you with the transferring." Beau drew it shut behind him.

Masters longed to throw the phone out of the window, but he didn't. Instead, he picked it up and called Ethan.

Ten minutes, later he'd been coached through how to transfer the information and was getting ready to contact the man he needed to when he came across an image of Anabelle Lee on his own phone. Taken in Russia, she wore all white, her red hair spilling down from her fur cap to stop in the middle of her back in a single tight braid. The only other color was the slice of black from the rifle strap.

Hot. Sexy. Mine.

Masters groaned and rubbed his dick through his jeans. He'd not seen or heard from her since she's departed his office upon her return from Chile. At least not in person. For sure as shitting, she made nightly appearances in his dreams.

He was so close to undoing the top snap on his pants and pulling his cock out to find some relief, but he had work to do. So he picked up his phone and made a call.

"Masters, long time no hear."

"Hi, Phillip. I need something."

"What's up?"

Phillip Taylor was another leader at Theta Corps, who operated on the west coast. He had a good division of agents under him and there was one particular person he wanted sent.

"I need Paula transferred here."

"Paula Shone?"

"Yes."

"Can I ask why?"

"I've got two agents down for a duration and she's a great person to help out. Plus she's worked with members of my team before."

"Did you give her a call?"

"No. I wanted to give you the heads up first. She's under your team and I didn't just want to yank her without you knowing why."

"Thanks for that, at least. We'll miss her. She just got back from a mission about two days ago and has been on downtime since. I'm sure she's ready to go. Do you need her number?"

"No, I have it, thank you. Have a good day, Phillip."

"Hey, is the rumor true that Anabelle Lee quit?"

"No, she's just taking a vacation."

"Good. I had the pleasure of working with her once, and *damn* is all I can say to that experience."

"Bye, Phillip."

Masters hung up before he could delve too much into what that 'damn' referred to. Had they slept together or was he impressed with how well Anabelle Lee did her job?

His mind had careened down a very dark road. Masters did his best to shake it off. By the time he'd finished the calls he had to make, it was time for him to head home. He'd gotten nothing else done and more work had piled up for the following day.

"How the hell did she do it all?"

He'd not even taken lunch and his stomach rumbled, reminding him a man his size needed to eat more than once a day.

"Mino," he called out. "I want takeout from that Asian place you always get it from. Same order and *goddamnit*, she's still not here."

He went through the contacts once more and paused when he arrived at what sounded like a restaurant. Dialing the number, he waited for it to be picked up.

"Golden Panda, how can I help you?"

"Yes, I'd like to place an order please."

"Are you wanting a repeat of what you usually get?"

"Yes, I would."

"We'll have it there in about fifteen minutes. Thank you."

He hung up. "Okay, guess they have the number flagged. At least I'll get some food."

He looked back over all the work he still had to finish just to complete the day and swore. It wasn't going to happen. Half of those people he still couldn't call because it was too late and their offices were closed.

There were some other things he could finish, but he still wouldn't be out of the office until past midnight. And he had to be in before six. He cut his gaze to the leather couch along the back wall.

"Hello, bed," he said with a sigh. While he waited for the delivery, he prepared the couch—it wasn't his first time sleeping in the office so he had blankets and pillows in the closet.

He'd just finished when security buzzed him.

"An order for you, Masters."

"Thanks, Johnson. I'll be right down."

"No problem, sir. I can bring it to you."

"Don't I need to pay for it?"

"You have an account with them, sir. They bill you. Mino set it up."

"Thanks, come on."

What does it say about me that security knows more about what goes on with my secretary than I do?

He met Johnson out by the desk Mino used to occupy, took the food and thanked him once more. Back in his office, he sat on the couch and spread the food on the table before him. His stomach growled aloud as he opened his General Tso's. Reclining, he used his chopsticks and filled his grumbling belly.

It was after two in the morning when he stumbled over to his temporary bed and flopped back. With a groan, he tugged a blanket over himself and closed his eyes.

Like usual, Anabelle Lee's image came to his mind and he swore before rolling over, trying to get a few hours of sleep. She wouldn't relent, staying with him, her long red hair barely covering her tempting breasts as she watched him with those cobalt eyes.

Fuck.

He slipped his hand below his pants waist and to the opening of his boxers. Staring at the ceiling, he pulled himself out and began stroking his cock. Gentle strokes as he slowed his breathing.

It grew with each tug and thickened until he was ready to slide between her firm thighs and have his way with her once more. He shut his eyes again, wishing she was with him instead of being just a memory.

Up and down his shaft, he moved his touch. Not as good as her firm hands on him, but he'd take it. He needed the release. Pinching the head of his cock to slow his release, he shifted on the cushions beneath him.

His memory was amazing, however. It took him back to Russia, where he'd gotten to touch her for real.

Where he'd been able to caress those breasts, suck them into his mouth and feel the silken glide of her hair along his skin as she sat on him, riding him, taking his cock so deep it wouldn't go any farther. The wet heat of her pussy gripping him, milking him.

"Fuck," he muttered, hips bucking up as his release hit him.

So much for taking the edge off. He wanted her more now than ever. After climbing from his makeshift bed, he walked to his private bathroom and cleaned up before going back to try to sleep again.

His alarm woke him far too early but he rolled from the couch, cursed over the stiffness in his body and readied for his day.

Three minutes after six, his phone rang. Rubbing the back of his neck, he padded to it and yanked it to his ear. "Masters."

"Oh, my god, I'm so sorry, sir, I thought I called Mino."

"This is her phone. She's not in today." *Or it used to be her phone.*

"I'm sorry. I'm here with your tuxedo for tonight's gala. She wanted to make sure it was correct before I left. Would you like to check it out?"

He didn't know this woman and had forgotten about the damn dinner tonight. *And here I'd been thinking how nice it would be to get out of here early and she came in early to make sure this was correct.*

"Bring it on."

"I don't have access. Mino came to me."

Not the way to start his day, especially without any coffee in him. "I'm on my way."

He hung up and went to the elevator. As it took him to the first floor, he tucked in his shirt and made sure the image he showed the outside world was the one he wanted them to have. He was in control and unflappable.

The woman waiting there was a tall brunette. Her brown eyes were kind even if she looked a bit sleepy.

"I'm sorry to make you come all this way, sir."

"Not a problem. Can I see the tuxedo?"

She unzipped the black bag she had been holding draped over one arm and took it out.

He took it from her and turned it around. *Like I know what the fuck I'm looking for.* "Looks fine, thank you."

"My pleasure." She reclaimed it from him and put it back in the garment bag. "Here you go."

"Again, thank you for bringing it over so early."

"It was when I could. I have a bunch of things to do for tonight but Mino asked me to make sure it was here this morning, so I adjusted my schedule."

"I appreciate it." Masters walked her to the door and sent a security guard outside with her to make sure she made it safely to her car.

He had almost gotten back to the elevator when someone called his name.

"Masters?"

Turning, he laid eyes on the blonde woman he'd been expecting. Paula Shone.

"With me," he ordered before pushing the button for the elevator.

Chapter Eight

The music to *Rolling in the Deep* by Adele woke her from the slumber that had cocooned her. Fighting a yawn, Anabelle Lee reached for the phone by her bed.

"Yes?"

Whether or not the word had come out like a word, or if it was more like a growl, she wasn't sure. And quite frankly, she didn't give a damn. She'd overindulged last night and her head pounded like the percussion section of a marching band.

"Anabelle Lee?"

The voice was small and frightened, all the while sending fissures of awareness down her spine, wiping away the lingering effects of her drinking. Only one person she knew had that voice, always cowed, always frightened.

Carlos' sister, Lewa.

"Lewa?" She sat up and shoved her hair away from her face. It fell back right away and she raked it to the side once more.

"I know I'm the last person you want to hear from but" — her voice dropped more — "I'm in trouble and need help."

"It was your brother I had issues with." *And killed.* "Not you. What do you need?"

"I think they're going to kill me."

"Who? Who do you think is going to kill you?"

"The same people who killed Carlos. They're after me."

Anabelle Lee got up from her bed and made her way to the office. "I can assure you that the one who did that to Carlos isn't after you, Lewa. But what people are you talking about? Do you have names?"

She plugged her phone in and began recording the conversation on the off chance she missed something she would have a copy to go over later.

"Lewa? Are you still there?"

She sent a text to her brother to have him trace the call on her phone then put it back to her ear. "Lewa?"

"I'm here. I had to wait for them to leave."

"Who? Who's with you?"

"I told you, the ones who killed Carlos."

She put in her handsfree device and ran back to her room to change out of her sleeping attire. "Where are you, Lewa?"

"Last place I recognized was Huétor de Santillán. I'm sorry, I didn't know anyone else to call." There wasn't any way to disguise the tears and fear in her words.

"Don't apologize. I'm on my way to you, Lewa. Listen to me, this is the most important thing I can tell you. Do what you have to in order to stay alive."

Typing fast, she put in the name Lewa had given her and pulled it up. It was a small town in the *Sistemas Beticos.*

"Tell me what you can, Lewa."

"They came in the middle of the night and took me. We drove a long time, I stole this phone from someone at a petrol station. I'm going to have to go, though, they don't give me much time alone."

"Okay, how many are there?"

She pulled a black Aerosmith T-shirt on over her head, readjusted her earpiece then yanked up a pair of cargo pants. Opening her closet once more, she then dragged out her olive-green canvas to-go bag.

"I've only seen two."

"And they told you they killed Carlos?"

She sniffed. "Bragged about it."

"And where did they grab you from?"

"My flat in London. I'd come home from work and they were waiting for me."

"This is what I want you to do, Lewa. End the call with me, do what they tell you to and every five minutes turn the phone on so I can ping it and pull up your location. I'm coming to get you, but I don't want the battery to die. So turn it on then turn it off after a minute."

"Thank you, Anabelle Lee."

They ended the call and she immediately reached out to Ethan. He answered on the first ring.

"Did you track it?" she demanded, hefting her bag and making sure the house was shut down.

"She's in Spain. The mountains."

"If there is a more specific location, I would love that."

"A lot of interference, but I'm running a few other things."

"Can you narrow the area for me?" She drew shut her door after setting the alarm.

"*Sistemas Beticos.*"

"That's what she told me." Flipping her keys, she jogged down to her truck and tossed her bag across the bench seat after opening the door. "I'm headed to Spain, house is locked up."

"What the fuck? Wait a second, Anabelle Lee. Who is Andy McDonald?"

"Who's that?"

"The phone I traced — that's the name it's registered to. Christ, what have you gotten yourself into now?"

"Gotta go, the phone will be on every five minutes for about a minute. Keep tracking it, I'll be in touch." She broke off and hopped in her vehicle.

Revving the engine, she tore out of her driveway and headed for the building she'd stomped away from all that time ago, unsure if she'd go back or not. But for Lewa she would without a doubt.

She pushed the speed limit the entire way there and squealed into her parking spot in the parking garage once she made it past security. Bag slung over one shoulder, she hoofed it to the elevator and pressed the button for Masters' office.

The doors hadn't even opened all the way before she was striding from the car to his office.

"Mino, I need to…" She canted her head to the left when she saw Mino wasn't at her desk.

Interesting. I don't think I've not seen her there.

She went to the door and knocked twice before pushing in. Her gaze swept the room and took in two things. One, she'd really missed looking at that man on a daily basis and two, he wasn't alone. There was a blonde in the room with him. They were close together, heads near to touching.

Anabelle Lee cleared her throat and the woman jumped back. Masters hardly moved. When she saw her face, Anabelle placed her. Someone she recognized from a previous op. Paula Shone.

Masters lifted his head and heat flared seconds before it got tamped back. "Knocking?"

"I did. You were obviously preoccupied."

"What are you doing here, Anabelle Lee? I thought you were on a vacation."

She tightened the hold on her bag and slanted her gaze to the woman in there. "Give us a second, Paula."

"Contrary to popular belief, Anabelle Lee, you don't run this office. We were in the middle of something."

"I'm not in the mood, Masters. Paula, leave."

Paula listened, closing the door behind her. Masters put his hands on the desk and pushed up.

"You have overstepped."

"Get over it. I need the jet."

His laughter had no humor in it as it flew like a shot from his mouth. "You don't get to issue ultimatums in this office, Anabelle Lee. I'm the one in charge," he said, poking himself in the chest.

"Are you going to give me the jet or not?"

"What's it for?"

"I need to get to Spain."

"No." He sat and laced his fingers.

"No? That's it?"

"Correct. No, I'm not helping you. It's not a Theta Corps op, you're not utilizing my resources so you don't get to use the jet."

"Because you need it?"

He shook his head. "That's part of your problem, Anabelle Lee. You think everything here is at your disposal and part of it is my fault for allowing you to get away with it because I'd been infatuated with you, but if you're not going to protect yourself someone should. So no. I'm not giving it to you. I'm not letting you use the jet for your own use."

Anger rushed her like a defensive end coming at her with one vision in mind. Taking her to the ground.

She whistled low and shook her head. "I never thought I'd see the day you sat by and let someone's life be in danger all because you want to throw some power around."

"You're not the only one who has things they want done, Anabelle Lee. But I'm not stopping my day just because you come bursting into my office and demand use of the jet."

Okay, so maybe I did that. "It's how I've always done things."

"And now that's not going to fly. You wanted to take a vacation, you're on one. Go enjoy it." He crossed his arms and stared back at her, no emotion in his dark gaze.

"And if I wasn't on one, would you have given me the jet?"

"No. Things have to change around here. You are getting too wild and out of control."

She checked her phone—no update from Ethan. "This is because of Russia? You're acting like this because you gave in and fucked me. Then you saw me dressing in slinky clothes and didn't approve, although when I first created that cover, I was told 'do what I had to make it work.' And I did. But now, you don't like it. You're some kind of fucking hypocrite. You know what? Fine. I'll save her without you. Without Theta Corps."

Anabelle Lee dug in her bag and dug out her identification that allowed her into the parking garage.

She walked to his desk and put it down in silence. One final perusal of him and she spun on her heels and departed the office.

Masters didn't take his eyes from the door until he could no longer see her. Only then did he glance down at what she'd put before him. Her access card to headquarters.

What the fuck did she give me this for? The second he asked himself that question, he knew the answer was the one thing he'd never wanted. Anabelle Lee had just quit.

"Goddamnit!"

He stormed back from the desk and went to the window. He peered down in time to see her black truck racing out of the parking garage.

He'd meant to set some boundaries, mostly for himself because he'd given in to her. And more often than not, her gut was right and he didn't mind that he'd given in. He, like every other person in the world, had an Achilles Heel and it was the woman who'd just left. Unlike most times, there had been no yelling — even when she called him a fucking hypocrite.

And she was right. I am a hypocrite. It was because of the clothing and the thought she may be having to sleep with another man. It tore me up inside.

He'd been able to handle a professional distance until that night they'd crossed the line in Russia. Ever since then, he'd wanted to protect her more, put her where nothing could hurt her. It didn't make sense, given the woman he'd fallen for was one who longed to be in the thick of the action.

He went to the phone and called Ethan.

"What's up, Masters?"

"Anabelle Lee. Where is she right now? Track her phone."

A pregnant pause. "What? Why?"

"Because she just quit and I think she's about to do something Anabelle Lee-ish."

"Something dumb then."

"Dangerous," Masters corrected. Dumb wasn't a word he equated with the woman. Himself, perhaps, but never Anabelle Lee. "Where is she?"

"Driving through town. What the fuck is going on? She texted me this morning to track a phone that called her. It was from a man in London, she said she didn't know. Then said the phone would be on every five minutes and to keep an eye on the location."

"Where was that?"

"Spain. What's my sister got herself into?"

"I'm about to find out. Do me a favor and call Mino. Tell her to come in and run the office while I'm gone."

"No can do, boss. She quit. Yes, I know. She and Rally are good friends so I found out."

"Damn it."

"What are you going to do?"

"See if I can keep your sister from either creating an international scandal or getting herself killed. Not sure which it's going to be yet."

"We can go. She's our family."

"No. I got this." He ended the call and ran for his own vehicle. He had a plane to catch.

It didn't take him long to locate the information about the flight she was on. He ensured he was one of the last to board, so she couldn't run and take a different flight. She was in first class and her expression told of her shock when he lowered himself beside her.

"What are you doing here?" she asked in a monotone.

Damn it all, he wanted more emotion from her. Hell, even the surprise at seeing him faded within seconds.

"Figured you would need some help doing whatever asinine plan you had gone about hatching."

"Can I get you a drink before we take off?" their attendant asked.

"Jack for me," Anabelle said.

"I'll have the same."

She nodded and moved on again, leaving them alone with each other on a plane of hundreds.

"Now, you want to help? I asked for help before."

"No," he said. "You didn't ask, you demanded."

"I always demand. But you've trusted me before."

"This is different."

"Right, and I forget." She paused when the flight attendant returned with their drinks. "Was that because we've fucked and now suddenly your *magic dick* made me incapable of doing my job and I now need a *man* to save me, or because I interrupted your time with Blondie?"

"The sarcasm I recognize, but that last bit, what was that? Jealously? Are you jealous of Paula Shone, Annie?"

She snapped her gaze to his, a mixture of hope, desire and anger flickering in the depths before it was masked. She blinked twice, slowly, and shook her head as she sipped her Jack.

"Not sure what I have to be jealous of. I told you after we slept together that it was what it was. Not making any claims, nor am I pouting if you decide to sleep with someone else."

Not what he wanted to hear. But he let it go because no matter what words fell from those ruby lips of hers, he heard the jealousy. And it was something he would address later. Right now, he needed intel on what the situation was they were heading into.

"Tell me what's in Spain, or rather who."

She handed over her empty glass and sighed. They backed away from the gate and taxied out to their place in line.

"Carlos has a sister. A much younger, very sweet, a bit slow, sister." She ran her hand down her pant leg and readjusted in her seat. "She — her name is Lewa — called me this morning and said the men who'd killed Carlos had taken her."

He furrowed his forehead. "The men who killed Carlos?"

"So she said. I asked her more than once, even tried telling her that no way the ones who had killed him were after her. But she said they'd told her they were the ones who had killed her brother. They took her from her flat after she got home from work. She snagged a phone from a guy at a gas station and called me."

"Why you and not the police?" He crossed his arms as they began gearing up for their own takeoff.

"Not sure. Maybe she thought the police wouldn't help her."

"My question is how does she know you can? Does she know you work for Theta Corps?"

"Worked and no, she wasn't ever told. At least not by me. I doubt Carlos did, he didn't have any use for her."

Masters had to swallow back his immediate response about refusing her resignation.

"Which brings us back to why she called you?"

"Because I'm pretty much the only family she has left."

"But you divorced that man. So, you're not family anymore."

She shook her head and stared out of the window as they climbed to cruising altitude. "I divorced Carlos, not Lewa. I enjoyed her company and found her to be sweet and unassuming."

He grunted and rotated his ankles. "Have you been in contact with her since the divorce?"

She clenched a fist before she relaxed her hand and rested it on her leg. "How is that any of your business?"

"I'll take it as a no, given your tone."

She ground her jaw and took a deep breath. "I don't have a tone and that doesn't change how you think this is any of your business."

"I'm making it my business. Don't even try to stop me from being here because I'm not going anywhere."

"Would that I could throw you out of the plane."

He knew she'd so it and opted not to answer.

"I know I'm the last person you want here, but I'm here. Let me help you. Trust me to help you."

"Why?"

"Because I'm here. I'm with you on the damn plane to Spain. Who else are you going to trust?"

He didn't want to hear her say another man's name. However, when she didn't respond at all but opened her blanket and covered herself, he wanted her to say something. She didn't, just closed her eyes and drifted off to sleep.

Once they hit cruising altitude, he connected to the Wi-Fi and began making some arrangements for when they landed in Málaga. She may think she didn't want his help, but she was going to get it.

After they woke for a meal, he tried again.

"How will you find her?"

Anabelle Lee nursed some tomato juice as they flew. He angled his body toward her, doing everything possible to keep their conversation private.

"I told her to turn her phone on every five minutes. Ethan's on it."

He nodded. "Is there any part of you that thinks she's in on this?"

"Of course, there is. I'm not a complete idiot," she said, turning the glass in her hand. "That was my first thought. But when she insisted on those men telling her the truth in regards to Carlos, I just, I don't think she is. Not that it matters. If she wants to deal with me because I did what I did, then that's something I'm willing to face. But if not, and she's truly in danger, I have to help her. She doesn't have anyone else. No one to check on her if she's missing, no parents to worry, nothing. Carlos was it, absent and indifferent as he was."

He closed his computer and replaced his tray table. With a yawn, he gazed around the plane. People were settling in for the night, those not sleeping already conversing in hushed tones. He opened his own blanket and draped it on himself.

"For what it's worth, I don't want you to quit."

"Already did." She put her pillow on his shoulder. "But there is a silver lining to it."

He didn't agree. "What's that?"

"Now we can fuck without you having any guilt over sleeping with someone in the company."

That shot lead into his cock. Masters couldn't even come up with any response until well after she had fallen asleep against him.

Chapter Nine

The wind whistled along the slopes of the mountains, spinning through the leaves and rustling the needles. Hunting birds lazily rode the air currents above them, piercing the day with their occasional sharp cries. The breeze was warm and held a hint of clean water and an earthy smell. She loved it.

Adjusting the backpack, she tapped her ear and waited to be connected with her brother.

"How was the flight?" he asked the second he answered.

"Long. Where is she?"

"Last ping was still in that same area of when she called you. I've pulled a few sat photos and there's a small cabin up in the mountains that I get five heat signatures in. One person in a room by themselves and the other four in the rest of the building."

She gazed over her shoulder at the man who'd invited himself along on the trip. Her ex-boss, Masters. *I can't lie, I'm glad he's here.*

He approached her, wearing dark blue cargos and a gray shirt that only amplified the strength in his body. She swallowed and focused on her brother instead of the walking sexy ad getting closer to her with every passing second.

"What's the verdict?" Masters crossed his powerful arms and took a deep breath.

"He's got satellite images. Ethan, send them to us. We're off to get a room."

Masters speared her with his gaze and she did her best not to tremble with needy anticipation.

"Will have them to you by the time you get there. Be safe." He was gone.

"What was the bag you picked up at the airport?" His question came as they headed for the rented convertible.

"Weapons."

"Weapons?"

"Look, I was coming here alone. I needed weapons. So I had a contact leave some for me."

"You've got drop caches everywhere, don't you?" He hopped into the passenger side and looked at her expectantly.

"Of course. Never know when cash or weapons will be needed." She started the engine and drove off to the hotel up in the mountains they were staying at for the night.

It wasn't a dive, but it wasn't a five-star resort, either. She didn't mind – it was quaint and she fell in love with it immediately.

As she took in the area, she spied some meandering trails leading off to who knew where, wildflowers growing in small tufts of grass and, off in the distance, low-hanging clouds moving in, covering the mountain tops as they floated. Had she the time, this would be a place she'd love to just explore for days on end.

They checked in and once in the room, she tossed her bags on the bed as he did the same with his own. She unpacked the guns and ammunition as he set up his laptop and grabbed the information sent by her brother.

As they waited for the pictures to load, he helped himself to half of her arsenal.

"Would you have taken all of these with you?" He loaded a Glock.

"Yes."

"Always have loved your guns," he commented.

She almost took offense but as there wasn't any rancor in the tone, she let it pass. "True."

Her phone rang and she put it on speakerphone this time. "What do you have, Ethan?"

"Get to your hotel?"

"Yes. Computer's up and running as well, just waiting for the images to de-pixel."

"Boss, Beau asked Mino to come back and she said no then kicked him out. Paula said she'd man the duties until you came back."

What the hell happened there? It rubbed her wrong to think of Paula there, but she couldn't worry about that now. She met his dark gaze and he arched an eyebrow in silent dare.

He gave her a slow smile. "Tell Paula I appreciate all she's done."

Anabelle Lee wanted to smack it off his face but she did nothing.

"Sure thing. Anabelle Lee, Beau says you need to check the bottom of your bag, something extra was put in there for you." He muttered to someone then came back. "Are the two of you going to be okay?"

"Sure thing," she said. "I have plans to fuck his brains out tonight then leave him in that comatose state as I go after Lewa."

"Christ, Anabelle Lee, I don't need to hear that. However, if he touches you again, I'll kill him."

"Roger that. I'll make sure to do all the touching in that case." She ended the call and tossed the phone to the bed as she went for the bag to pull up the bottom.

"I'd laugh but I'm not sure you weren't kidding about that statement." He approached her. "What's in the bag?"

She smiled and withdrew out a pair of handcuffs. Dangling them from one finger, she winked at him. "Does it count as only me touching if you're cuffed?"

Masters quirked an eyebrow. "Let's find out."

In the next heartbeat, she was in his arms as his mouth slammed down on hers. Wrapping her arms around his neck, she hooked one leg around his waist, bringing him in closer.

Their tongues dueled, teeth hit and lips mashed as they struggled for dominance of the kiss. His taste flooded her and she whimpered. Desperate need she'd been keeping locked up in a tiny box in the corner of her mind for this man escaped and took over.

They were frantic in yanking off each other's clothes. Items went every which way, but finally they were naked and he had her back on the bed, pushing into her core with a fluid motion.

"Fuck, yes," she cried, arching into him, taking him deeper.

"Annie," he ground out by her ear seconds before he nipped the lobe and sucked it into his mouth.

Goddamn it, she'd missed hearing him call her that. It didn't matter how good he helped her feel, that name from his lips—well, it made her feel unique. Special.

"More." The word fell from her lips as a plea. "Oh, Jesus, please, give me more."

He complied.

Back and forth he stroked his length within her, catapulting her to a higher plane. She wound her arms under his shoulders so her nails bit into his muscles. Each forward thrust pushed her farther up the bed. Legs hooked tight about his back, she took what she needed from him and asked for more.

"Fucking shit, Annie. You're killing me here."

She wasn't doing any better where she lay. Her belly clenched at his calling her Annie. He was the only one she would ever allow to use such a name with her.

"So tight."

In and out. She closed her eyes and gasped as he yanked on her hair.

"Watch me. I want your eyes on me. I'll be damned if you think of anyone else while my cock is in you."

She allowed his gaze to swallow hers. Like anyone else could make an appearance in her mind when she was with him, hell, she thought about him if they weren't even in the same room. As his hips drove his dick home over and over within her, she never looked away. She felt him everywhere. Her skin burned from the intensity between them. The room grew hotter and hotter until she wanted to burst into flame.

Anabelle Lee undulated her hips and rolled them as he continued to thrust. Her internal muscles clenched and released as she came. Back bowing, she cried out as he followed her over the precipice.

Their bodies coated in sweat, he grabbed her hips, keeping himself buried deep inside her. Anabelle Lee didn't make him ask. She took over and began riding him. She stared down at the man beneath her. On either side of him were guns and ammunition. Toward the top of the items sat the handcuffs her cousin had given her.

Reaching for them, she gasped at the touch of his mouth on her nipple. He laved it and rolled the tip with his tongue before grazing his teeth along the sensitive bud. She clicked the metal around his wrist and brought it up to the headboard, then she did the other one.

He watched her without blinking.

"I could leave you right now," she panted.

"If I thought that would happen I wouldn't have let you cuff me." He bucked his hips and she mewled in pleasure. "Let's enjoy tonight, Annie. You and me. Nothing else. No one else."

Lowering her face so her hair fell in a curtain around them, she licked his lips. "One night. One more night."

As she captured his mouth, she didn't think about anything else.

* * * *

"Ideas on how to cross without walking through the freezing mountain water?"

Masters slanted his gaze to the woman beside him, hands on hips as she gazed over their latest obstacle.

Damn it, she's gorgeous. Khaki cargos cupped her ass in the most tempting of ways. A green shirt seemed painted on over her curves. Black boots and that stunning red hair of hers spilling down her back in a loose ponytail.

Hair he'd had on his chest last night while she'd blown him more than once.

"Nope, can't say I was expecting this river to be raging with snowmelt. There were some rocks a bit farther upstream. We could go there and cross them."

"Lead on."

As they walked, he couldn't disagree with the raw beauty of where they were. When they'd arrived that morning, the grass had been silvered with frost, reminding him that while it was warm during the day, it was still cold overnight.

They got to the rocks and he shook his head. "No fragile ice or anything to make it easier?"

"Find your big boy pants, Masters."

"Not what you said last night. Pretty sure you wanted me to keep my pants off."

"I also said one more night. That was then, this is now."

She could turn it on and off just like a damn light switch. Right now, she was all soldier.

They hopped over three of the slick rocks — well, she managed four. She turned to him and cocked her head to the side.

"What?"

"What's your name?"

He blinked. "You know my name."

"No, I know what people call you. What's your name?"

She leaped to the next one and his breath caught as she wobbled. Once she'd regained her balance, she glanced back to him. "Well?"

She pitched her voice to carry over the river and he jumped to the rock she'd just vacated.

"I don't share my name."

"Who am I going to tell out here? Hell, we have three more rocks to make. I may die before this is over. Tell me the name of the man I spent the night with."

"Major Stacey Erkens is my full name."

She turned back to him and, before he could say anything, she leapt back to the rock he stood on. It was barely big enough for him and he grabbed her tight to keep them both there.

"Is that a military title, Major, or first name?"

"Are you insane? Why did you jump back over here?"

"You wouldn't have let me fall in." Absolute confidence in her tone.

"We both could have gone in."

"Nope. You have a good stance there. I checked before I came back over. Were you wobbly like on the last rock, I wouldn't have. Answer my question."

"First name."

"Who gave you the nickname?"

His brain shorted out when she slipped her arms around him beneath his coat. "One of the kids in primary school. Billy was his name. We were the only two there of Native American blood and we got picked on a lot, so he decided I should be called Masters so people wouldn't pick on me."

"Did it stop?"

He thought back. "Yes, but not because of the name."

She tipped her head so she could meet his eyes. "You fought them, didn't you?"

"I did."

Her smile melted the ice he'd put around his heart so long ago. She'd managed to ingratiate herself to him from day one, with her own ice-cold demeanor, steadfast loyalty and sharp tongue. After dressing another man down, she'd looked at him and winked, no shame in her behavior and that had been it. He 'd been lost.

"Why are you smiling?"

She leaped to the next rock, with no wavering this time.

"Annie?"

She turned her head and beckoned. "I think I have you figured out."

He snorted. "Not a chance."

"Oh, I'm confident." She moved forward to the next one and the last before the ground, then hopped over to land on the soft earth of the riverbank.

He followed.

She set off and he reached out and snagged the end of her ponytail, drawing her back to him.

"How confident?"

"More than you think I should be. Come on, we still have a few klicks to hump." She tried to turn back but he held her still until he got a kiss.

Anabelle Lee nipped his lower lip then skirted away before he could deepen it further.

They set off at a slow jog, heading up toward the coordinates Ethan had last provided them with. It was easy moving with her. They kept conversation to a minimum but when it flowed between them there wasn't any forcing of words. She was easy for him to talk to.

"Can I ask you something else?" She grabbed her water bottle and took some water.

"It's your dime." He propped a shoulder against another tree and watched the sun turn her hair into a deeper burnished copper instead of the bright red he was used to seeing. He liked this richer color.

"What's going on with you and Mino?"

"She quit."

Anabelle Lee spat out the water and sputtered. "What? What the hell did Beau do to her?"

"While I'm glad you think it wasn't me that did something to her, but I think it was my fault over Beau's and I hate to confess that."

"You?" She shook her head, disbelief all over her face. "What would that even be like in the realm of our reality for you to do something to her? She's your stabilizing force, your calmness."

Not really, Annie, that job is yours whether you want it or not. "I pissed her off, pushed her too far and she quit."

"So, basically, what you're telling me is, you opened your mouth and said something male." She cocked an eyebrow.

He scowled at her. "Stop acting like women don't say stupid shit."

"Never said we didn't, but let's not think y'all don't corner the market on stupid shit said. Especially to women. Did you apologize to her?"

Masters harrumphed and lifted his binoculars and scanned the landscape.

"Oh, my fucking God. You just let her go. Listen to me. You're never going to find another one like her. She runs your office and I'm guessing you are realizing just how much above and beyond she went for you to ensure seamless operation. You should get her back unless you're just too proud to tell her you made a mistake and you want her back. Of course, I wouldn't say you want her back to run the office, tell her you want *her* back."

"And that works?"

"It would for Mino."

"That your way of saying it won't work for you?"

"I'm not coming back to Theta Corps. I refuse to be there when I'm treated like I suddenly can't do my job."

"I allowed my emotions to cross the line."

She waved him off. "Don't. Just… Don't."

Damn it, he had to fix this. "What if I told you I don't want you to leave?"

"I can't, Masters. Don't ask it of me. Right now, I have to focus on myself and I can't do that if I'm jetting off around the world to save others."

"That's what you signed up for."

"I know." She took the nocs from him and used them. "This way. I see a small tendril of smoke rising above the trees. I also know that because I have things to work through, I'm not going to be at my best and that's not fair either to the ones I'm out to help or my teammates."

He caught the item she tossed at him.

"What about your brother and cousin?"

"I don't speak for them — you'll have to ask them. My guess is Ethan will not be in the field as much but will still do your computer stuff. Beau won't change. He's always been the wildest of us all. I'm tired."

He gripped her arm and turned her toward him. "Of?"

"Seeing the faces and eyes of the dead each time I close mine, waking up at night from nightmares. Seeing that face on the young boy I just killed recently. I can't get it out of my mind," she rasped, tears filling her eyes.

The sight of the first tear floored him. She was so strong. She got angry and fought, she screamed and yelled. He'd never seen her cry, not even the time they'd thought Ethan had been taken from them forever. But here and now, seeing the start of tears for a boy who, had she not taken the action she did, would have killed her cousin.

Masters began to draw her closer, but she shook her head and removed his hand from her arm. "I don't have time for this."

He kept his counsel. This wasn't the time for snark or for him to try to console her.

Gesturing for her to lead on, they struck away once more. This time, she didn't stop until they saw the cabin in the distance. A long, narrow one-lane road led to the building.

They shared a look and split up, the plan already in place. She touched her ear and within moments, Ethan's deep voice filled his head.

"Same number as before, no one has come or gone."

"Any on the approach?" he asked, moving into his position.

"Negative. You have a clear path."

"Thanks, Ethan."

"Keep my sister safe." He was gone before the response from Anabelle Lee, or himself, could come.

I have no plans on losing her now.

Chapter Ten

The rough bark of the tree dug into the flesh of her face. Anabelle Lee didn't move. It wasn't comfortable and she longed to move, but that wasn't an option. She even ignored the small part of the branch jabbing into her left breast. Which was also very uncomfortable.

They'd spent the majority of the day hiking up here and now they were waiting for the shadows of night to come and helped them blend them in upon their approach. There wasn't any noise from the cabin. No one left, no one drove up. There wasn't even any yelling.

She ran over Masters' question about if she doubted Lewa. *If she was tied or beaten she wouldn't be able to scream and try to escape. Then again, not everyone is like me and fights all the time.*

She'd thought about it. She knew this young woman and hoped to hell it wasn't a trap. She would tell her about Carlos but, in all honesty, this wasn't the best way for it all to come out if she didn't already possess the knowledge.

She shivered inside her jacket as the night air replaced the warmer air. Checking her watch, she began moving at the prearranged time. She didn't have to check to see if Masters was coming.

He was.

The man might have been in charge of them all, but he still got his hands dirty in the field if necessary. And she was glad he was with her on this. Walking ball to heel, to ensure she made no noise, she crept to the closest window and peered in.

The men there were heavily armed but there was no sign of Lewa.

She ran a hand over her mouth and withdrew a flash-bang grenade. Hand on the trigger of her sidearm, she made her way to the only door and waited. Seconds later, Masters tapped her on the shoulder.

Counting down from five, she popped it, opened the door and threw it in. She and Masters turned and covered their eyes. As the pandemonium began the two of them burst in.

It didn't take them long at all and she pushed into the back room and froze when she found Lewa curled up on the floor in a small ball, shivering and crying. Holstering her sidearm, Anabelle Lee pulled her close and hugged her.

"I'm here, Lewa. You're safe now."

"Anabelle Lee?"

"Right here." She ran her hands up and down her back. "They can't hurt you anymore."

"I don't understand why they wanted to take me. All they talked about was you and Carlos. And how they'd killed him."

"And wanted to kill me?"

She sniffed. "Yes."

"They didn't."

"But my brother."

"Carlos is dead, Lewa. That wasn't a lie, but they didn't kill him."

In the low lighting of the room, she glanced up at Anabelle Lee. Her large brown eyes were red and puffy from all her tears.

"How do you know?"

"I was there when he died."

"We're clear here." Masters stuck his head in the room briefly.

Anabelle Lee got to her feet, encouraging the woman to rise with her. She did so on shaky legs and it took her a bit to get them under control. Lewa held her tight as they walked to the room, although it wasn't warmer by much.

"Who's he?" Lewa asked as Masters tossed Anabelle Lee a blanket.

Wrapping it around her thin shoulders, Anabelle Lee patted her in hopes the blanket would help warm her faster. "A friend."

"He looks serious," she whispered.

"He is." She glanced across to where Masters kept an eye on the windows.

"We have to stay the night here and go in the morning. She won't make it out there."

"Agreed," she said. "There was a small bed in there but not much in the way of coverings. Anything else she can have to cover up with that you saw?"

Masters brought in a thick jacket and a pair of woolen socks. Anabelle Lee didn't want to ask where he had gotten them. She had a good idea — off one of the dead men. If Lewa knew that she didn't state anything, just put the items on, then wrapped the blanket back around herself.

"Think the wood will last all night?" Anabelle tucked Lewa in on the sofa, putting as much warmth on her as she could. They'd even moved the couch a bit closer to the fireplace.

"If we use it sparingly, we should be fine." Masters checked his ammunition then moved back by each of the windows, checking. "Get some rest. I'll take first watch."

Anabelle Lee didn't argue with him, just nodded and climbed onto the couch with Lewa, sharing her body heat.

No matter how hard she slept, her eyes popped open the second Masters touched her shoulder. Carefully, she extracted her body from Lewa, tucked her back in then yawned.

"Anything?" she asked, taking her hair down for a moment, rubbing the back of her head then putting the ponytail in again.

"No, it's been all quiet," he said.

She checked her watch. They had two hours before sunrise and this was the time she would be assaulting if it were her. Most people were sleepy then, groggy if they were even awake. Dusk and dawn, were the two best times, she'd found.

"Go. Rest. I've got this."

She checked her weapons and watched him put a bit more wood on the fire before making his way to a chair. Seconds later, he was sleeping.

They had a breakfast of cold MREs before leaving. Without a vehicle, they had plans on getting back down to the inn where they'd been staying. From there, they would get her back to London.

The trek was slow—Lewa was still not that good on her feet and a lot of people didn't hike in the mountains much less after being held prisoner for a while. They moved with her between them, alternating on who was point and who was rear.

On one break, she stood beside Masters, hands resting on her M-16. "What do you think?"

"I think we're going to have some problems when we try to cross that stream. She's weak. She can't jump from rock to rock. We have to have to carry her. I will, I mean."

She stared at the map in his hands and angled her head. "Think we could find another place to cross? One that may be simpler?"

"Any changes will add on to our time out here. We don't want to be here overnight without shelter. Do you think she could make it even farther?"

"She doesn't have a choice. She wants to get off this mountain and back home, then she's going to have to dig deep if that's what's called for." She drummed her fingers on the stock of her rifle.

He nodded. "Your mission, your call." He folded the waterproof map and shoved it in one of his many pants pockets. "I'll take point." He walked off before she could say anything else.

"Come on, Lewa. Break's over."

She rose and took off after Masters without a word. Anabelle Lee paused over where she was sitting, making sure there wasn't anything left behind that could be used to track them, or any indication of where they were heading. She was still unsure about the situation.

Nothing happened on their way down and she didn't relax her guard until Lewa was in the shower at the inn and she was alone with Masters.

"What's up?" he asked, packing his bag.

"Didn't that seem a bit too easy to you?"

"Compared to some of the missions we've been on, yes, but this was a kidnapping that they didn't appear to have planned for."

"Exactly. I don't know. Never mind, I'm sure it's nothing."

"Don't push away your gut, Anabelle Lee, it's rarely wrong." He shouldered his pack. "I'm going to arrange for some transpo and get us home. Back soon."

She nodded and sank to the bed when he exited.

Lewa walked out of the bathroom shortly after and looked even younger in the clothing she'd borrowed clothing from Anabelle Lee. It was too big on her.

"Better?" Anabelle Lee patted the mattress beside her.

"Warmer, at least." She sat and rested her head on Anabelle's shoulder. "Why would they take me?"

"I don't have a clue. I don't even know who they are. Did you overhear anything else?" Ethan was running prints from the men they'd taken out at the cabin but she'd not heard back from him yet.

She shrugged. "I don't know. I was so scared." She laced her fingers together. "How did you know they didn't kill him? I know you said you were with him, but did you see the shooter?"

Dread welled up in her chest. "Yes."

"Who was it?"

Anabelle Lee looked at the woman she'd always liked. "I did it. I killed your brother."

Lewa stared at her as if the words didn't quite make any sense to her. Or perhaps they were rearranging in her mind to make sense. Either way, the blank look existed and in the depths, Anabelle Lee could see her working it out.

Slowly, she drew away and stood, tucking her dark brown hair behind her ear. "You did it? You killed my brother?"

"I did." *And I won't offer any apologies for doing so.*

"Why would you do that? I know you didn't stay married to him, but he was a good man. He loved you."

"It's not that simple, Lewa."

She struck, her hand connecting to Anabelle Lee's cheek with fiery purpose. "You bitch! I hate you and I will never forgive you for this."

Anabelle Lee stood. "Fine. You do what you think best, but remember this. I had already killed him when you called me asking for help and I didn't come out of guilt, I came because *you* asked for my help. He wasn't what you make him out to be, he never had time for you. You had your one swing. You take another and I will hit back. Go get your shoes on. We'll be heading for London soon."

Lewa ran off at the mouth in a flurry of Spanish curses. Anabelle Lee didn't do anything more than point back to where her footwear waited.

She fought the urge to rub her jaw. Lewa had put power behind that hit. It was going to be a long trip.

* * * *

Anabelle Lee followed him in silence up the steps to the waiting jet. Masters had noticed the difference between the two women as they got on a plane for London. Anger and hatred burned in Lewa's gaze and there was cold acceptance in Anabelle Lee's.

He nodded at the other agents on the plane. They were catching a ride back with other members of Theta Corps. He wasn't down with that flying commercial bit. They watched him as the highest member of the company. He commanded respect wherever he went. Plus, there were the rumors about the redheaded woman with him. So there was awe between them both for these younger agents to absorb.

Anabelle Lee strode for the back and claimed a seat. He sat across from her.

"Everything okay?"

"Ready to get home. I don't suppose any of your private stash is on this plane, is it?"

His heart skipped a few beats at the twinkle in her eye. He leaned forward. "You do know that's *my* stash, right? I mean, it's not for everyone."

"But you have such good taste."

He raked his eyes over her. "Yes, I do."

True to form, she didn't blush or even get flustered. She leaned forward as well and stated in a low tone so no one else could overhear them, "Careful now, don't want those youngsters spreading rumors."

Somehow, he didn't give a damn.

"Give them something to talk about during the flight."

She chuckled and reached for her phone. When she plugged in some headphones, he knew he was about to lose her for the flight. He held up a hand, stopping her in the process of putting in the earbuds.

"Yes?"

"I'm sorry about your relationship with Lewa. I know that wasn't easy for you."

And the walls went up—he could see it plain as the nose on her face.

"She deserved to know the truth and when she asked me I wasn't about to lie."

"But you liked her."

"I still do. The important thing is she was rescued and is fine. How she feels about me now is irrelevant."

"No, it's not. But I'm figuring you out, as well, Anabelle Lee. I'm figuring you out." He sat back and straightened his legs.

On the flight back, he spent time talking to some of the other agents onboard with them, as did Anabelle Lee. He saw her engaging in a few conversations, but for the most part she kept, to herself, earbuds in and either sleeping or listening to music. He didn't blame her nor did he try to push her into doing more. She tended to keep more to herself, as she always had.

He reviewed cases with some of them and just gave advice on many things he'd picked up on over the years. When they landed, he was the last person off, right after Anabelle Lee. He spied the vehicle waiting for the others, saw one for him, then there was Beau who sat on his motorcycle, waiting for his cousin.

"Thank you," she said as they headed down the stairs to the tarmac.

"For?"

"Helping even though you said you weren't going to." She paused at the bottom and faced him. Looking up at him, she gave him a small smile. "You know where to find me." Then she wheeled back around and headed to where her cousin waited for her.

While he may have wanted to remain where he was and watch her walk away, he couldn't. That wasn't something he should be caught doing. Especially with a dick as hard as the surface he stood upon. Therefore, he made his way to the idling SUV.

"Home, sir?" the young man asked as he climbed in.

"No. Take me to Mino's."

He didn't have to give directions as he'd gone there many a time before. He had to get her back to work.

He found a cold bottle of water waiting for him and uncapped it to drink. Then he rested his eyes until they pulled up to the apartment complex. He took a deep breath as he waited for the man to open the door once more.

"Give me a bit."

"Yes, sir."

Masters stared at the building and shook his head. *I should have moved her to a better place a long time ago. No reason for her to remain here. I pay her more than enough to get in at a better building.*

He strode through the door and went to the single elevator bay. There were no security cameras anywhere he could see. The elevator light was flickering when he got inside.

Another mark against the place. He'd not been here in over a year and didn't like how the area hadn't improved, but had in fact declined.

He stepped out on the fourth floor and glanced along the hallway. Dingy carpet, but at least it wasn't littered with stains. He walked down to her door and reached up to knock, only to hesitate.

Why am I hesitating? I want her back and I definitely need to make sure she's doing okay.

He knocked and waited.

The door opened and he found himself face to face with Mino. Her black hair was in a long braid and she had on a pair of pink pants with baby-blue paw prints. Her shirt was the opposite.

"What do you want?"

"Why are you still living here? I pay you enough for you to be somewhere safe."

"Goodbye, Masters." She swung the door shut.

He swore and stopped it from closing. "I'm sorry. That's not what I came for."

"If you came to get me back, that's not going to work, either. I'm done."

"May I come inside?"

She rolled her eyes and sighed. "Whatever."

He entered and smiled. That was more like it. Her place was spotless. "I came to apologize."

She crossed her arms and lifted one arched eyebrow. "What for?"

"What I did to piss you off and make you leave."

Her gaze narrowed and an unpleasant feeling snaked up his spine.

Mino walked to her kitchen and propped against the counter. "Be specific."

"About?"

"The apology."

"Seriously? Why are you being this way?"

"Because I don't think you know or even give a damn about what it was you did. And until you can tell me what it was you did to hurt me, take your apology and your arrogant ass out of my apartment."

"Don't get emotional."

She pushed away from the gray countertop, moving closer to him. "Don't get emotional? Is that what you *just* told me?"

"You know what I meant. Mino, you're not someone I want to lose at work. Come back and we can forget this whole incident."

"Maybe you should learn to be a bit more emotional, then you'd be able to keep the woman you've been pining over for years. You're heartless, Masters, and I'm not coming back to work. Find someone else."

"Don't want the pay, fine." He stomped out, more pissed at himself than her.

The door slammed behind him and he fought a wince.

Way to go. Be a jackass once more.

The elevator opened and he stepped in only to whip around and stride back down the hall. Oh hell no, he wasn't going to leave it like that. Not happening. He pounded on her door and she yanked it open.

"What?" she demanded.

"Here's the thing," he said, crowding her so he could come inside. "I look at you like a little sister. *My* little sister. One I need to protect. Have since I got you there. So when I fuck up, I expect you to take it with a grain of salt and keep on going. I am who I am and you know this. Have known it. I haven't changed. I am a hardass Neanderthal of a man. I get it. And you, you're not."

She blinked. "Thank you. I'm glad you've noticed I'm not a man."

"Mino." Her name flowed from his mouth on a thread of warning.

She appeared nonplussed. "Carry on."

"I don't know what I said. I don't know what I did. I have a lot on my plate and —"

"Don't."

He shook his head. "Don't what?"

"Use your busy life as an excuse for being an asshole."

"You and Anabelle Lee, never afraid to call me out on the carpet."

"Well, you can practice with me and get it right for when you go to her. Although she'll most likely take a different kind of apology that wouldn't work for me."

He glared at her and she sneered and rocked back on her heels.

I'm not addressing this right now. Have to focus on fixing this with her.

"Fine. I'm sorry, for whatever dumbass thing I did. I want you back, I need you back."

"I know you are. You probably didn't even realize you said it. However, my terms still stand."

"Very well." He went to the door and stepped in the hall. "I still want you out of this building, Mino. It's not safe." He closed the door behind him and left. "Home."

"Very good, sir."

Mood sour, he counted the minutes until he reached his place and could relax.

Unlocking the door to his home, he sighed in relief. All he wanted was a hot shower and a drink. A large, stiff one.

He dropped his bag off in his bedroom and made his way to his bathroom. Stripping, he then turned on the shower and waited for it to heat. Not wanting to spend that much time in there, he climbed out and dried off before tying a towel around his waist and making his way back to the rest of his place.

Masters paused, for there, standing at his bar, facing him with two drinks in hand, was none other than Anabelle Lee.

"What are you doing here?" He somehow managed to squeeze the question from between his lips. All the blood rushed south and that didn't do much good in the line of forming coherent thoughts.

"Offering you a drink," she said, one hand outstretched with the tumbler filled with amber liquid.

"Annie," he growled, his leash on his rabid control near to snapping.

She sipped from her glass then walked to him. "So, how'd your chat go with Mino?"

Masters took the drink and slammed it within seconds, the burn bringing tears to his eyes. Single malt wasn't meant to be drunk in such a fashion.

"I'm not talking about that right now."

She took another drink—not a tiny sip as if she were scared of it, a drink that showed she loved what was in the glass.

"What are we talking about then?"

He placed his empty glass on a flat surface. "How fast I can fucking get you naked, Annie."

Chapter Eleven

Anabelle Lee didn't feel half as confident as she pretended to be. She hadn't wanted to be away from him tonight so she'd come to his house and let herself in as she had that first night she'd snuck in. But this wasn't about getting rest before she dashed off to somewhere else — this was all about getting sex.

More of that mind-numbing, body-pleasing activity she had found no one else could come close to delivering on as he could. She finished her drink and put the glass back on the beautiful teak bar.

"I'm fast. How about you?"

Masters crooked his finger at her and pointed to the bedroom. She smiled, heat spiraling up from her belly and spreading throughout her body.

She captured her lower lip in her teeth and smiled saucily. "I mean, are we timing it? Is this like a race on who can get naked the fastest? Are we putting money on it? I think I could beat you. I'm not wearing panties, so that's one less thing for me to remove."

His jaw clenched and she watched as his Adam's apple bobbed with his swallowing.

Gotcha. She sucked her lower lip into her mouth and shrugged. "But since that would have meant I wasn't matching, there's no bra either." She gestured to her sheath dress. "So it's really just this and my shoes." Anabelle Lee turned her back to him and gazed over her shoulder. "But it's okay. It does have a zipper if you'd like a go at that."

He made a fist, then relaxed his hand. "Get out of your clothes."

"No. You said you wanted to see how fast you could get me *out* of them. So do it."

God, she wanted to tempt him further, see him rush to her, push her up against a wall and fuck her until she couldn't walk.

She pivoted until she again faced him. "It's going on two minutes since you issued that challenge. You're not very good at this. Do you need help? Are you slowing down in your old age?"

The rumble left his chest as he was on her. There was a loud rip as the material of her dress tore, leaving her in only her three-inch heels. Masters ran his large hands over her naked body and lifted her so the remnants of her dress pooled where her feet had been.

Seconds later, his cock pushed at the entrance of her pussy and she purred as he thrust inside her wet heat. Using the wall to support her, he began to move.

Her toes curled inside her shoes and she tightened her hold around his waist. Having him deep inside her, filling her, stretching her. There wasn't any single word to explain how that was for her.

He surged forward and she gasped. "I think we can improve on your time. It may take a while, but we can do it. May need a lot more practice."

Masters dipped his head and captured a nipple in his mouth. Tremors shot through her once more as he flicked his tongue over the tip in time with his thrusts.

"Fuck!" she cried, scrabbling for purchase with her hands on the wall behind her.

There wasn't any and so she gave up on the wall and took hold of the man keeping her there. His muscles danced beneath her grip, rippling with the raw power he had contained within him.

"My thoughts exactly," he muttered.

Words failed her. Failed him. All that was left between them were the grunts and moans of two people sharing in the pleasures of their bodies. She came twice against the wall and he moved her to his couch, pulled out, turned her and slid home from behind as she was bent over the leather back.

She woke a while later, wrapped by both blankets and his warm body. Anabelle Lee yawned and shifted against the wall of muscle beside her.

He tucked her closer and placed a kiss on her temple while he smoothed his hands along her naked skin. Wriggling her feet, she realized they were no longer confined in her heels.

"When did I lose my shoes?"

"I took them off when you jerked in your sleep and damn near punctured me with one heel."

She smiled, but didn't move away from his chest. "Sorry. I can kiss it and make it feel better if you'd like me to."

"Nothing on me hurts, but I'll never say no to a kiss. Would you like to know where you got me?"

His teasing question had her chuckling. She smoothed one hand down his chest, over his taut abs and on to capture his cock. "Here?"

He bucked his hips and nodded. "Yes."

"I'm more than happy to inspect it and make sure no damage was done. Also, make sure I sincerely apologize for almost injuring it."

"Him," Masters said.

"Excuse me?" She drew back to look at him this time.

"He's a him, not an it."

She rolled her eyes. "Does *he* have a name, as well, or should I just call him Masters Junior?" She began stroking his length.

"We prefer *His Illustrious Emperor*, but you can call him MJ for short."

"How about I call him mine and leave it at that?" She swiped her thumb over the large mushroom head, smearing the pre-cum.

"Sounds perfect." He threaded his hand back through her hair and pulled her closer for a kiss. "Fucking perfect."

Her stomach growled and she sighed. "I need sustenance."

"What are you hungry for?" He ran his hands over her skin as she continued playing with his dick.

"What do you have?"

"Not much. I don't eat here much."

She snorted. "Are you even here much?"

"No."

"Yet you have this beautiful place?"

"It's an apartment. Nothing more. Not home."

"Where is a place you consider home?" She moved her hand faster and tightened the grip.

He moaned and shifted against her. "I don't know. Haven't found where I want to be yet." His words had become breathy and drawn out.

"That's too bad. We should all have a spot we like to be."

He slid a hand between them, cupping her pussy before slipping two fingers inside her. "I do have a place I like to be. Very much."

She nipped his chin. "I meant for a permanent home-type place."

"Details, details." He pumped his fingers and she rolled more to her back, giving him better access. Re-angling her hand, she captured his cock once more and began jerking him off.

"Fuck, you're good at this," he grunted.

"Not too bad yourself." Heat unfolded within her and moved to every part of her body, increasing as each pump of his fingers drove her closer to that ever-desired edge of reason. That place in the world where she lost sight of everything but the euphoria soaring through her, where nothing mattered but pleasure. Where nothing else existed.

He put the pad of his thumb on her clit and rotated it. That was all she'd been missing. She exploded into tiny fragments of light.

"So fucking gorgeous when you come," he uttered seconds before claiming her mouth in a soul-stealing kiss.

Anabelle Lee pumped his shaft even as he came hard with a guttural groan. She'd barely come down from her own high when he picked her up and carried her to the shower.

Twenty minutes later, they stood making a late-night meal. Breakfast. She kept an eye on the omelet while he chopped some fruit to go with their food.

Anabelle Lee couldn't keep her focus off him. Masters had on only a pair of pants, which hung low on his lean hips. The dark gray material didn't even begin to hide the large cock he had and that was where her gaze continued to drift, all without any prompting.

Christ, I'm pathetic. Thinking of that sliding back into me. Over and over again.

Even so, she didn't let the food burn. She'd been cooking far too long for that to happen.

"Plate?"

He slid it toward her with a push from the knife handle he used. She grabbed it and hefted the pan with her other hand, before transferring the food onto the white surface in a smooth motion.

As she carried it to the table, she yawned then looked around his place. There wasn't a lot to give away any insight into the man who lived there. He was a private man.

He joined her moments later and kissed her cheek as he bypassed her, placing the bowl of grapes, strawberries and apples beside the omelet. With his other hand, he dropped some silverware.

"Looks delicious," he said, pulling out a chair for her.

She smiled as he pushed her in before taking a seat himself. This hardcore man had more manners than many she knew. That to her was one of the sexiest things every. Manners could make or lack of, break, her opinion of a man.

They didn't speak much during the meal or the cleanup. She'd just finished the last dish when his phone rang. With a wink, he reached for it and answered.

Two seconds later she gathered that the news, whatever it was, wasn't good. His expression darkened and his body stiffened. He gave a few orders then hung up. Her nerves lit like the sky during the Fourth of July.

"What's going on?"

"You coming back?" he asked.

"No."

"Then I can't discuss Theta Corps business with you."

This was no longer the lover, but the cold asswipe of a boss. He left and in moments had reappeared from with a dark blue button-down and black slacks.

"What's happening?"

"I'm leaving. Stay as long as you want. I don't know when I'll be back." No emotion, no anything but business.

"Masters."

"No!" His singular barked word took her aback. "You quit on us. You don't get to know. Now, if you'll excuse me, Paula is waiting for me."

And the dagger sank even deeper between her ribs into her heart.

"Well, by all means, go running to her then," she snipped.

He paused as if he were about to say something, shook his head and left the place. Leaving her alone.

"Fuck!" She slammed her hand on the countertop before dropping the towel over its hook.

Within minutes, she had left his place and was headed back to her own. Her insides were a churning mess. She wanted to know, wanted to be part of the action.

It was my decision not to be there anymore. And while she understood the code of Theta Corps and that they didn't share with outsiders what was going on, it still irked the hell out of her. She had been one of them for years, fought beside them, bled beside them. And now, *now*, she was outside looking in.

I don't like this.

* * * *

Masters swore as he stood before the large screen projecting the image seen from the body camera Beau wore. The night vision view wasn't fun for him to look at, not from this end. His palms burned. He wanted to be out there with them.

"Clear," Beau said softly, his drawl familiar and calm. *Don't know if I'd ever known him not to be calm.*

Jason tapped him and moved by, taking point. Masters was on pins and needles. This job had zipped down to hell about fifteen minutes before Paula had arrived to pick him up. She'd driven him right back to their HQ where the two of them had gone to Subbasement Two and pulled up the feed.

Someone had ratted them out and the men were pinned down, trying to find an escape. In the back, the sounds of automatic gunfire could be heard. At times, it would get louder then fade when the trio running got more distance between them and their pursuers.

Paula was in the room with him, mimicking his stance, eyes firmly on the screen before them.

"When did you get the call?" he asked her, muting his link to the men on the ground.

"Right before I came for you."

"It's a fucking dead-end," Beau rasped. "Anyone got any C-4 left? We can make a door."

"If we blow this, it's going to flood with water." Another voice filled the room—Jason, from the sound of it.

Beau cycled his weapon and turned to face the other two men. "We all know how to swim. We can't stay here. We'll be cut down. It's our only option. Make it so."

"Is he serious?" Paula asked him.

Masters nodded without taking his eyes from the large screen. "This man rarely jokes about getting out of a situation alive."

"So instead of heading back to engage the enemy, he's going to blow a hole in a wall, allowing freezing water to flood. That's insane."

Masters cut his gaze in her direction. "They're low on ammo, won't make it back through the gathering men after them. This way, they have a chance." He released the mute button. "I'll have a pickup for you at exfil two. Get out, swim up and north six klicks."

"Roger that," Beau said.

The third member, Tim, set the charge and they all backed out of the blast zone.

"Fuck," Paula whispered.

He agreed, but didn't say a word. The explosion sent debris past the camera lens and for a moment, their sight was obscured.

"Go, go, go!" Beau commanded.

"You can't wait here," Jason's voice reached them.

"I'll bring up the rear. Get going and get to where Masters stated the pickup would be. Move."

When the smoke cleared, Masters watched the water come rushing in and he knew their sight was about to be cut off. Beau tipped the camera toward him and flashed a grin along with a thumbs-up. The scruff on his face and the do-rag on his head combined to make him look dangerous and adorable all the time. There wasn't fear, but excitement.

Then he was gone and seconds later so was their live feed.

He looked at Paula. From the uncertainty in her expression, she wasn't the one he'd be adding to the team. Sure, she was good in the field, but the look she had currently, would have been nothing but a disaster for the ones on the ground.

"Let's go," he said, wheeling and striding to the door.

"Where are we going?" she asked, right on his heels.

"Catching a flight." He stopped and looked back at her. "Is that going to be a problem?"

"Not at all. I have a go-bag in the building."

Yes, good agent but not one I'm putting with that team. "Good."

He didn't say anything else as they headed for the helicopter pad. When they were in the air, he called to have the jet readied, so they could take off as soon as they got there.

They hustled onto the jet and buckled in as they taxied. Their pilot was amazing and got them up in very little time.

Ignoring Paula, he rose and headed to the bar. As he checked the cabinet the first thing he saw was an open bottle of his single malt that shouldn't have been there.

Anabelle Lee.

As usual, she took what she wanted and did as she pleased. His lips curved up in a smile before he caught himself and wiped it away. However, he did pour himself a glass of it. Then he went back to his seat.

"How do you know if they made it out of the hole and survived the water?"

He sliced his gaze to her. "How do we ever know? You've been in situations like this before, yes?"

She nodded.

"This is business like usual."

"I've not been in situations like *that* before."

He knew that and it added to his reason for not having her join Beau's team. They were his best, his top operatives, and most situations got sticky. If this was her behavior from the safety of an airplane or a basement room, she didn't need to be in with the rest of them.

"I appreciate you coming to help, Paula, but I'll be sending you back to your unit after we get done with this op."

She straightened. "Was it something I did?" A frown. "Or didn't do?"

"No. I only had you temporarily. It's time for me to get you back to your team."

"Oh," she said, shrinking into herself.

It irritated the fuck out of him. Anabelle Lee would have been arguing with him the moment he'd told her she was being sent elsewhere. But not this one. Paula was taking it.

There's something wrong with me if I'm upset this woman is showing me the respect I've earned.

Paula rose for a bottle of water then sat back across from him. As she cracked the top, he sighed.

She just wasn't the fit he wanted. Yet he waited, for her to argue for herself, attempt to get another shot, find out what she could do. But Paula didn't do or say anything. That disappointed him. He'd thought she'd been made of sterner stuff.

His frustration grew and corkscrewed to Anabelle Lee. She was the one who made him this way. The one who'd ruined him for this job, had him expecting more from all he met. And it wasn't happening.

He clenched his fingers around the glass then took another long drink. There wasn't enough alcohol in the world to ease his budding anger. Paula didn't talk to him. She remained silent and focused on the stuff in front of her. He'd left a file on the operation there and had no problem with her looking at it.

By the time they were preparing to land, they'd both been over the file. There'd not been any contact from Beau and he wanted to hear from them, find out if they'd all made it. He and Paula disembarked and headed to the waiting vehicle.

As the driver rushed them along to their next destination, she looked at him. "Something on your mind, Shone?"

"I know why you're sending me back."

He glanced over to Paula. "I already told you."

"No, I know what this was. It was a test."

He crossed his arms. "A test?"

"Yes. Everyone knows Anabelle Lee quit and you need someone to be on your team. I didn't make the cut."

"Who told you about the rumor she quit?"

Paula lifted one eyebrow and shook her head. "I'm not blind or deaf. You have rumors flying around there about how she walked out on you and the company."

He ground his jaw. "I see."

"So, I failed and I know this, but I want to know why."

"Okay, you were panicked when you saw what Beau, Tim and Jason were going to do. It was all over your face. You wouldn't have been an asset but a hindrance, were you there."

"So, I've never been in a situation where I had to blow a hole in the wall of something underwater, to flood it, just so I can hope to get out alive."

"No need to be defensive. You asked. That's the point. This is something he wouldn't bat an eye over having to do. You wanted to go back the other way, which was a sure death. This way, there's a chance."

"So I'm not brave enough."

"You're a damn good operative, Paula. Which is why he has you on his team. You have to be in order to be there for Theta Corps. But working with Beau, that's an entirely different level. When they go out it's because we know something is going to go wrong, it's not going to be a smooth rescue or operation."

Her skin flushed and she struggled not to lose her temper. He knew because he made it a point to check everything about the ones he was thinking of having on his team.

"So because I questioned his actions, I'm out?"

"Because *when* you questioned him there was doubt in your tone. You have to trust, fully, the men you are with. Your action proved you didn't."

"Because I asked a question?" Her control slipped and her voice rose.

"Yes. Because you thought that it would be better if they went back the way they'd come, because you didn't trust Beau to know his actions were in the best interest of the group. You said his actions were insane."

"I won't again. If given another chance."

"You don't have another chance. When we're done, you go back to the West Coast."

She scowled and he turned away from her, done with the conversation. Paula stayed at his side, but didn't speak unless spoken to first. Masters knew she wasn't happy with his decision but he wasn't there to make people happy — he was there to keep the people of his country alive.

Even so, he couldn't explain his relief as he laid eyes on Beau himself, coming off the transport. He arranged for a car to take Paula back to where she needed to go then had their ride refueled for the trip home.

He waited until they were airborne before he snagged a seat beside Beau.

The country boy cracked his neck and rolled his head to look at him. "What's swimming around in that head of yours, Masters?"

"How'd they do?"

"Fine. They are used to doing things a different way but they are good. I have no problem working with them again."

Masters frowned. "That's it?"

"Unless you'd rather talk about you fucking my cousin."

Masters wished for another drink, perhaps this time, a double.

Chapter Twelve

"Are you ever going to go back to work or just do nothing but this painting thing for the rest of your life?"

Anabelle Lee glanced away from the easel and, after flicking a swift gaze to her grandmother, who still sat in her rocker, quilting, stared at her brother. "Ethan, shut up."

"Manners." Grams never looked up from the quilt as her reprimand fell.

"Grams, he has no right to ask me that," she protested.

"All she's doing is sitting here sulking. She needs to be working."

"I don't need my brother sticking his nose in my business and trying to tell me what I need to be doing." She gripped her paintbrush and counted so she didn't chuck it at his head.

"Get over yourself and go apologize to Masters. He'll give you your job back."

"Damn it, Ethan. Enough. I'm not going."

She slammed her brush down on the ledge with enough force that the entire thing rocked and crashed to the ground. Her paint spread all over the canvas she'd been working on, the red staining the white magnolia petals she'd painstakingly painted much like blood inching across the once pristine ground.

Anabelle Lee stared at it before looking at her brother. His face mirrored the shock she felt. She didn't like to have outbursts like she just had.

Grams put down her quilting and sighed. "Red paint doesn't look all that good on my porch." She got to her feet. "I expect it cleaned up and you two to work out whatever this is going on between you. This behavior isn't how you were raised, much less act with each other. You're family, so start acting like it."

She walked away, leaving them alone.

Anabelle Lee hopped off her stool and glared at her brother. "Look at what you made me do."

His eyebrows shot up. "Excuse me? I made you do this? Act like a high schooler? Throw a tantrum?"

"Fuck off."

He shook his head. "Don't take it out on me because you threw away your career."

"You don't have any idea what I'm doing, so let's not pretend otherwise." Her rage boiled to the top and she kicked another thing of paint, adding to the mess already created.

"What the hell is your problem?"

"You know what? I don't have one. You do — ever since you and Rally were stating you were engaged, everything is nothing but roses and champagne for you. Do you know what it's like to know who you want and can't? Of course not, because you have the one you want. Stop spreading your fucking sunshine on the rest of us. Sometimes we just want to be upset."

He furrowed his forehead and reached for her. "Wait a second."

She countered his move and brushed by him. "Go away." She hopped off the porch and strode to her bike and climbed on.

"What about this?" he called after her.

"Clean it up and throw it out, I don't care." She rode away.

Back at her house, she put her bike on the rack and went to the basement. *Grams is going to kill me. I can't believe I left her front porch like that.*

In her workout room, she grabbed the tape and sat on a bench by the wall. With some loud music playing, she wrapped her hands then feet. With a few deep breaths, she jumped up and began going after the free-standing heavy bag.

Sweat drenched her when the music stopped and she panted while looking around. Her brother stood there, hands stained red.

"You and I need to talk."

Wiping the back of her hand across her forehead, she cleared her throat. "Go away, Ethan."

"Fuck that. I just spent over an hour cleaning up Grams' porch with your paint all over it. Got my ass reamed by her and I'm not letting this go. She's right, we are family and you need to stop hiding behind, well, whatever you're using here." He gestured in her general direction.

"I don't need you trying to make my life what you think it should be."

"I know, and I've been an ass of a big brother." He approached her but held up his hands when she backed away. "Christ, Anabelle Lee, we're family. You are supposed to be able to count on me no matter what. So you didn't tell me about marrying Carlos. I can't forget that. So you volunteered to go off with him to save me. I can't ignore that, either, and while I was scared as fuck something would happen to you, it didn't. There are days when I forget you're not my baby sister who I have to protect all the time. You're a grown woman who can hold her own against any threat."

She didn't move and watched him. He never came closer to her. "Is there a point?"

He jumped at her, wrapped her up and took her to the mat. "Nope."

Anabelle Lee grunted as they hit the ground. "Then what the fuck was that all about?"

"It's about me needing my sister back. Rally is part of my life, yes, but I hate this chasm between us. We're family, always will be and I'm worried about you."

She rolled him off and jumped to her feet, circling him. "I'll make a deal with you. You beat me and I'll talk. I beat you, you leave me the fuck alone."

He toed off his shoes and beckoned her. "You're on. One stipulation, though."

"Which is?"

He cracked his neck. "I want to know what happened between you and Masters."

Just the man's name and she almost fell to her knees. The smile from her brother alerted her that he'd seen her falter.

Shit just got real.

* * * *

Masters sat in the tall leatherback executive chair before his desk. On the other side stood two new members. Rick 'Rose' Larson and David 'Fox' Hardison. They watched him with impassive expressions.

He was pleased these were the two he'd decided on to pair with Beau. Tim and Jason were good, but not good enough. These two were.

"Congratulations on your new assignment. It takes a lot to get to this division of Theta Corps."

"Thank you, sir," they both replied as one.

"Beau will be in later this afternoon to meet with you again and show you to your area. Get acquainted. Do you need to find housing in the area?"

"We have places," Rose said.

"Very well. You'll start some training once he arrives. This is different than other sections—we train harder and more often. There are situations when you'll be unable to contact loved ones for a decent amount of time. If you need letters written beforehand, I suggest you do so and find someone who will mail them for you. We have people on the third floor who will be happy to do that for you—just tell them when, where, and where the letter is coming from. They'll handle the rest. Is there anything I can answer for you?"

"I heard about Anabelle Lee. Is that a rumor or will we be able to meet her?"

Masters hated the admiration in the man's voice and it took all his control to keep his possessiveness out of his responding tone. "She's no longer at the agency, so you'll not be meeting her."

Fox looked at his friend. "Unless we run into her at a bar. I heard she loves to drink."

Masters cleared his throat and both straightened up. "Sorry, sir," Fox said.

After Beau came and retrieved them Masters turned his focus back to his computer screen and a file Ethan had sent him. Information dug up on The Watchers.

"I thought we got rid of this fucking group," he groused, slamming his hand on the smooth surface of his desk. "Montana? What the fuck are they doing there?"

"Better question would be how they survived."

He looked up to see Ethan strolling into his office as if he had every right to be there.

"Is knocking something that's not done in your family?"

Ethan grinned. "We knock when we should."

"And my office isn't a 'should' zone, is that it?"

"Pretty much." He sauntered all the way in and kicked the door shut behind him. "This is important."

"Secure important?"

At Ethan's nod, Masters flipped the switch that turned his office into a SCIF — sensitive compartmented information facility. Neither of them spoke again until the red lights along the top of his office walls were lit, indicating lockdown had been secured.

"What's going on?"

Ethan sat across from him and sighed. "After we lost Lexy to The Watchers I've been going through all the information repeatedly, searching for what I had missed. My being taken put a bit of a damper on that, then Rally came along and I had new information to scan." He cleared his throat. "Bottom line is, when I combined all that information, I found something I think is going to be useful."

"Which is?"

"Can you pull up the information on Trevor Mansfield?"

Masters did and slid the keyboard over to Ethan. The room was silent for a moment except for the sound of his fingers clicking over the keys at a fast speed.

"When I checked previously, all things pointed that this bastard was an only child."

Dread began filling his gut and Masters adjusted his seat, waiting for the other shoe to drop. "And now?"

"He's not a single child. In fact, he's a twin."

Masters shot forward. "What?"

Ethan put up the birth records. "He was a twin and his twin is still alive. In fact, they both are. And his brother is the one who was behind all the planes going down and Rally's kidnapping. Sure, Carlos played a part in it, but it's the brain child of these two men."

He sat there, absorbing the news Ethan had shared with him. Twins, a child who wasn't reported as having lived. Hell, he wasn't reported as having even existed. It explained so many things and yet made it all so much worse.

"Do we know where they are now?"

"No. Not either of them, I'm still running facial recognition on footage from Montana to see if he is spotted in the state."

"Keep me appraised on that."

"Always. There's something else, too."

Masters wiped a hand across his brow. "What's that?"

"This isn't a bad thing. More of an invitation."

He sketched an eyebrow. "For?"

"My wedding."

He smiled. "You two set a date finally?"

Ethan nodded. "We have. June, and we'd like you there with us."

"I wouldn't miss it for anything."

Ethan's smile could only be described as a man in love. While Masters was happy for him, he wasn't able to ignore the bit of him that was jealous he wasn't with the one woman who made him feel. Not any special way but feel on every basic level.

Anabelle Lee.

"Wonderful." Ethan got to his feet and stood by the door.

Masters flipped the switch disengaging the security on the room. Only once the red lights were gone could he open the door. Without a look over his shoulder, Ethan vanished, leaving him alone in his office.

He ran a hand through his hair and leaned back in his seat. Mansfield. *Had I never heard this man's name again it would have been too soon, and now, to think he has a twin psycho out there to help him do crazy and insane shit, doesn't make me feel any better.*

Masters grabbed his phone and pressed a preprogrammed button. With a heavy exhalation, he waited for the call to be answered.

"What do you want?"

"Some people say hello, Anabelle Lee, when they answer the phone."

"So call them."

He frowned. "Did I call at a bad time?"

"You called from your office, which you do when you want something from me. I no longer work for you or that company so yes, it's a bad time."

"Do you have time to come in and speak to me for a few minutes?"

There was a slight pause but she said, "Fine. I'll be in this evening. Goodbye." She hung up before he could say anything else.

He stared at the handset for a few moments before replacing it on the base. "Feisty."

A word that was a mild description of the woman he'd just spoken to. Anabelle Lee was a fireball — no, she was more than that, she was a sky full of them. Dangerous and beautiful at the same time. But this time, there was something in her voice he didn't like. No teasing, no fun, no *her*.

"Call for you on line four, sir."

His new secretary called out to him via the intercom.

"Thank you." He shook his head. Lucy was good but she was no Mino. "Hello?"

"Masters, this is Shady McValle, do you remember me? We've met a few times and I was at your party you had recently."

"Sure, I do, CIA. What can I do for you?" He didn't have much use for The Company but got along with Shady.

He chuckled. "I called to say thank you. I don't need anything."

"Thanking me for what?" He picked up a pencil and doodled on a sheet of paper by his hand.

"For Anabelle Lee Jackson."

Masters froze, stared at the pencil in his hand and blinked as the top half fell to the desk rolling until it hit his blotter. He'd just snapped it into pieces. "What are you talking about?"

He put into practice his ability not to have emotion in his tone — not an easy feat, because he wanted to growl, snarl and threaten the man for those words coming from his mouth.

Lucy stepped in and he waved her away. She nodded and closed the door behind her on the way out. He put the broken pencil in the trash as he waited for an answer.

"She didn't tell you?" Shady cleared his throat. "I thought she had. She's coming to work for my company. I wanted to thank you for introducing us. It was years ago, but you sent her to talk to us about some sensitive information and I was her contact. So, thank you."

"Sure thing." He couldn't bring himself to say 'you're welcome' because he didn't want her going there and he sure as fuck wasn't happy she was leaving without telling him.

"I hope we can get together the next time I'm in town. Have a great night." Shady hung up.

Masters hung up softly. He was anything but calm. He longed to toss his heavy oak desk out the window and do some redecorating in his office by way of a few holes in the walls.

He didn't do any of that. He sank back and drummed his fingers on the desk for a moment before jumping back into work. He would address it when she came in.

Then you can explain to me, Anabelle Lee, why you are leaving us for the CIA.

Chapter Thirteen

Anabelle Lee waved at the security guard sitting at the desk as she approached.

"Ms. Jackson," he said with a smile. "I'm glad to see you again."

"Hi, Keith, good to see you. I'm here to see Masters."

He nodded. "I'll take you up. We have orders to just bring you right on to his office. It's weird knowing you don't work here anymore." He got out from behind the desk, his stride a little off because of his prosthetic foot, but he still moved smoothly.

She didn't comment, just walked beside him as he escorted her to the elevator and the top floor. They exited and she saw an unknown woman sitting in the spot Mino used to occupy. Green eyes watched her as they approached the door. The woman didn't seem all that impressed or happy to see her.

"He said for you to go on in."

Anabelle Lee didn't feel the need to respond to her. She looked at Keith and smiled. "Thanks for the escort."

"My pleasure."

She popped a piece of gum in her mouth, crumpled the wrapper up in her hand and strode to the door, entering his office without knocking first. Masters sat behind his desk, hands clasped on the blotter before him, the typical scowl present on his handsome face. She lobbed the balled-up wrapper toward the trash can and smiled when it went in.

Blowing a bubble, she then popped it and said, "You wanted to see me."

She longed to go to him, bend over and touch everything on him. Or sit on the desk and unbutton that damn shirt of his, slide it back over his broad shoulders, then kiss everything she could reach. Then again, sitting before him and letting him push up her skirt, expose her panties to where he could drag them down and began eating her needy pussy…

"Close the door."

I would love to have this mean what I want it to mean. Alas, I'm sure he's all about work right now. He's got that damn scowl in place.

She turned and went back, nudging it shut with the toe of her heeled boot. "I don't have a lot of time, so are you going to let me know what this is about?"

He rocked forward and she had to derail her thought train of what it would be like to straddle his lap in that chair and ride him to orgasm. Masters stood and walked around his desk, stopping to perch on the edge. He hooked his ankles and crossed his arms. All that did was draw her attention right back to his physique.

Masters leveled a dark look in her direction. "Kind of pointless now, or so I just found out."

"I'm too tired to play games, Masters. What are you talking about?"

"I got off the phone with Shady McValle."

Fuck. She blinked and popped her gum before striding to a vacant seat. Smoothing her skirt, she sank to the cushion and shrugged. "Okay." *I will not let him see me rattled.*

"That's all you have to say?"

"I don't give a damn who you talk to. Is that all? I mean, we could have discussed this fascinating bit of information on the phone." She focused on his face, memorizing each and every plane of his face. "Did you miss me so much you had to call me in here for such a flimsy excuse?"

"You're going to sit there and act like you've not just signed on to work with The Company?"

Okay, so perhaps I could have told you, but damn it, it's not your business. She flicked a piece of imaginary lint off her brown skirt.

"It's the CIA and, what, I wasn't supposed to entertain any other jobs? I quit here. You, as my *former* boss, have nothing to say if and who I apply to work for. It's not any of your concern."

"I told you I wanted you back at work."

She shook her head, tucking a strand of hair behind her ear.

"Nope. I told you, I refuse to work with you and you behaving like a fucking Neanderthal, I'm not doing it. This work was stressful enough without having to deal with your jealousy."

Look at me being all adult and keeping my cool. Not an easy feat for her, at all, because she wanted to jump

back at him. That had been their relationship, going
head-to-head all the time. She was tired of doing it,
which was part of why she wasn't coming back.

"I'm not jealous."

Her eyebrows rose with doubt. "Right, of course not.
But somehow after you got into my pants you had an
issue with the clothing I wore or how I handled things.
I don't need you questioning my every move. I had
proven myself repeatedly during the years I was with
Theta Corps. I'm not a rookie, and I refuse to be treated
as such."

He frowned. "So, you're going to the CIA?"

"Why not? I'm good at my job and why not go
somewhere my talents will be appreciated?"

Anger flickered in the depths of his dark eyes.
"Including in bed?"

Well, hell, so much for keeping my cool. She shot from the
seat and marched right up to him. Her heels and the
fact he sat propped on the desk gave her a height
advantage.

"Are you implying I'm sleeping with people I work
with in the CIA? Shady? Is that what this is?"

A sardonic grin lifted one half of his mouth. "You
slept with me while we worked together."

Crack. She smacked him across the face. "You
arrogant bastard. Arrogant, egotistical, fucking
bastard." She shook, her fury was so great.

"Truth hurt?"

"No, and in case you'd forgotten, I didn't sleep with
you for years. And apparently doing so was one hell of
a mistake." She leaned in closer. "So, if I am stripping
down for Shady, it's not any of your business. If I want
to bend over in his office and take it up the ass, you

don't have a goddamn right to say a motherfucking thing about it."

His dark eyes flickered with dangerous flames. "Don't push me, Annie."

"My name is Anabelle Lee and you no longer have the right to call me Annie."

He stood, forcing her head back in order to maintain eye contact. "I'm the only one who has that right. And if you take him to your bed, I'll kill him."

Her pussy pulsed with the proprietary claim he'd just slapped down. She narrowed her eyes and stepped forward until she couldn't go any closer because of the heavy desk between them.

"You don't have any claim over me, and after I walk out of this office, we won't have anything to say to one another ever again." She pivoted and strode away, not looking back.

Anabelle Lee never made it to the door. His grip was firm around her wrist as he spun her back to him. She swung and he countered before sinking a hand into her hair. She snarled at him and his response was to kiss her.

Masters slammed his mouth on hers, taking what she would never want to give to another. With his left hand, he yanked up her skirt and palmed her ass.

She moaned, bucking against him, wanting whatever she could have for one last time. She nipped at his lip and scored her nails down the front of his shirt to stop on his zipper. The sounds of the metal teeth opening over the sharp, rasped breathing between the both of them.

He lowered his other hand and lifted her as he backed them to the wall. She freed his cock and pumped it twice, loving how it pulsed and jumped in her hand.

He bit the side of her neck then claimed her mouth in another bruising kiss. "Put me inside you so I can fuck you." A bite on her lip. "I'm going to fuck you so hard, you'll never not feel me inside this pussy."

She lined him up and pushed the head against her. He entered her in one thrust.

"My pussy," he growled.

Anabelle Lee didn't answer him. She couldn't find any words. His shaft filled her and she allowed her eyes to roll back in her head as he did as he claimed he would. Fuck her. Hard. Relentless. Unforgiving.

His muffled roar was delivered along neck as he pumped thick ropes of cum deep inside her. She shuddered as she came again and again.

He pulled out of her and stared with that blank, unforgiving stare. Her heart plummeted to the floor. He wasn't going to say anything else. He'd said it all — in his mind, she belonged to him.

Tears burned the backs of her eyes and she hated that. There wasn't any reason for her to be crying over him. He wanted to own her, that was all. Nothing else. Dictate what she could and couldn't do. She didn't roll that way. She'd been independent far too long.

Fixing her skirt, she turned away and walked to the door. *No more.*

He called her name but she didn't stop — hell, she didn't even slow. The wait for the elevator was tense and she just wanted to get the fuck out of there. Once she made it back to her vehicle, she headed for the one place she was always welcome.

Her grams had just removed an apple toffee pie from the oven and had coffee waiting in the pot.

Anabelle Lee hugged her grandmother, holding her tight as the familiar and comforting smell wound around her.

"How do you always understand how to make me feel better, Grams?"

"I raised you, chil'. I know all there is. Even when you think to keep things from me."

"You know I'm leaving."

"I *know* you're running from a man. You need to check your ego or you're going to end up alone."

"It's not that simple, Grams."

"Sure, it is." She released her granddaughter and pulled a knife from a drawer.

Anabelle Lee sighed and went for the mugs. As usual, she grabbed the ones she'd painted magnolias on. *Back when I was idealistic and hopeful for a different life.*

"No, it's not. I love him, Grams, but I refuse to be with a man who thinks he can tell me what to do and what to wear."

"Were those his exact words?"

She poured the coffee. While she loved her grandmother, there were times she felt the woman was still back in a different time when it wasn't unheard of for men to instruct their women on how to dress.

"It was implied."

Grams cut into the warm pie and put a slice on each plate. "Which means no."

"Grams, it's not so simple."

She slid a plate toward Anabelle Lee and harrumphed. They each carried their drink and pie to the table.

"I'm going to miss this," she said, enjoying a forkful of pie.

"It will be here when you come back. You're not selling your place so we get you will come home. Do you know how long you'll be gone?"

"No, ma'am. But as soon as I know, I'll let you know."

They finished the rest of their food in silence. As she carried the dishes to the sink, her grandmother got to her feet.

"Come back to the room you grew up in, Anabelle Lee. I have something for you."

"Be right there."

She wiped off her hands and walked down the hall to find Grams sitting on the edge of the twin bed she used as a child. Beside her sat a folded quilt. Grams had her hand on it.

"This is for you. Take it with you to wherever they send you. I'm sure you'll have an apartment somewhere."

"Can I see it?"

Grams stood and handed her one corner. Together they opened it and spread it over the bed. It was much larger than the twin but there was no disguising the beautiful job she'd done in completing this item.

"My magnolias, some of my favorite colors and music?"

Grams smiled. "Yes."

Anabelle Lee hugged her. "Thank you so much, Grams. I love it. I'll definitely take it with me."

"Do me a favor, chil'."

"Of course."

"Stay safe. Before you had family watching your back, now you're on your own."

A statement mimicking her own fear. But that wasn't something she was going to let her Grams know. She and the boys had a pact not to worry the woman who had taken them in when they all lost their parents.

"They'll take good care of me, Grams. But I will be extra cautious and careful."

They shared another hug and she gathered her quilt and left. Back at her house, her brother and cousin were there, waiting for her on the front porch.

No one said anything. Beau held up a bottle of whiskey and, together, they all went in to celebrate and say their farewells.

* * * *

Masters turned up the music, sending it blaring through his place. Music was his solace. Always had been.

But right now, it wasn't soothing him as it should have been. In fact, nothing did. Not since she'd left.

"Fucking CIA."

He closed his fingers around the longneck he'd yanked from the fridge earlier. Four months since she'd smacked him and left his office. Two months of trying to get in touch with her after allowing a cooling-off time. None of his attempts had been successful and she'd not once gotten back to him to answer any of the messages he'd left.

The doorbell chimed and he went to answer it. Ethan stood there, his laptop in hand. He didn't ask if he could come in, just brushed by and let himself through the door.

"Come on in," Masters remarked.

"I will."

He took a long drag of his drink. "What brings you here? I thought you were out of the country on family business."

"Came back. I've been unable to get in touch with my sister."

Unease churned in his gut. "Not my business. She doesn't work for me anymore."

"No, she doesn't, but she is my family and I'm going in to help her out. The fucking CIA is disavowing her."

"Already? What the fuck did she do?"

"She did her job and what they sent her to do. One of their supposed top agents died, but not before he betrayed her."

He placed the bottle on his table. "Take what you need and go. I'll be in ops. Pull Beau and take him with you."

"Where are you going?"

"To have a chat with the CIA."

"You're not coming with us?"

"No. I will be by after you bring her back, but right now, I have someone I need to have a conversation with." He used the remote to shut off the music and got his shoes. He and Ethan went down together and as they parted, he grabbed Ethan's shoulder.

His man turned to him.

"Yes?" Both his eyebrows had ridden so far up they were beneath his hair.

"Whatever it takes, you bring her back. I'll sign off on it."

"You know you should just tell her you love her. It would make everything so much easier."

Masters pointed off down the road. "Go." He was going to take it as Ethan's blessing, but again, something to think about for later. At that moment, he had to get to Langley.

He climbed into his vehicle and called his pilot on the way. He would fly up and have a vehicle waiting to take him to their building. There wasn't any point in changing prior, given he had more suits on his jet.

The plans had already been filed and all was ready by the time he got to the private airstrip. Jogging up the stairs, he didn't wait for the pilot to shut the door and he took care of it.

"Let's get going," he called out.

"Roger that, sir. Just waiting for clearance."

"As soon as possible." He claimed a seat near the front and stared out of the window at the waiting runway.

It didn't take them long and they taxied down, turned and took off. Once they were airborne, he left his seat and changed into one of his dark gray suits. The flight was short and the town car waited for him as he disembarked. The driver didn't speak to him, just held the door and closed it behind him.

The same when they arrived, no words were spoken. He just walked up to the building and entered, crossing the huge CIA crest on their floor. Flashing his badge, he got through security and was in the elevator for Shady's office.

The journey down the hall didn't do anything to calm the anger pulsing through his veins with each pump of his heart. Shady's office door sat open and Masters knocked on the frame before entering and kicking it shut.

"Masters." The man leaned back in his chair, the smile on his face just begging to be punched off.

"Tell me it's a lie." Those five words were dragged up from his gut, laced with danger and raw fury.

The man threaded his fingers and gave him a look Masters had no doubt meant 'I barely know you, don't ask me for any favor'.

"I don't know what you're talking about."

He took another two steps toward him. "Don't bullshit me. We both know what this is about. And by your sorry-ass attempt at a deflection, I'm going to assume *you* did this and it's not a lie."

The gaze became calculating and colder than he'd ever seen on Shady. "You need to keep out of CIA business."

"Fuck you. You recruit her, send her into a shit situation and when one of your own, older members betrays her before his death, you disavow her? Seriously?"

"She knew what she was getting into. She accepted the danger."

"She didn't know you were sending her into a volatile situation with traitors. And now you have her labeled as one?"

"We didn't label her as a traitor."

Seriously, this fuck wants to argue semantics with me? Fine. "True, you just yanked all her options away for getting any help from the ones who dropped her in this situation."

"Again, she had advanced knowledge what she was going up against. Besides, you had her on your team so you must have thought she was capable enough."

"She's more than capable and she will make it back. Now when she comes after you because of the shit you handed her, don't blame me. You brought it on yourself. You should have known better. You should have offered her support."

He snorted. "We weren't even supposed to be in the country. You would have done the same."

"The fuck I would have. I don't leave my assets without backup. I wouldn't ever yank help from one behind enemy lines. But then, that's the difference between Theta Corps and the useless CIA. We take care of our own."

"Had *you* taken care of her she wouldn't have come to us."

No disguising the meaning there.

Masters counted to ten and strode to the desk, bent over and snatched Shady from his seat. "Listen to me and listen well. She's going to get out of there and she's coming back to work with us, but you *will* send her whatever compensation she may need because of the stress you put her under. And I suggest you make it a damn good one. Remove the 'disavowed' tag and make her disappear from your files. She didn't work for you. Give her the money and forget she exists."

He clawed at Masters' grip. "Why are you here?"

"I told you, I don't like one of my people being treated this way."

"She left your company." He pounded on Masters' arm and he dropped him, unceremoniously back to the chair.

"No matter where she goes," he said, heading for the door, "she's still one of mine."

"You make it sound like she's your woman."

Masters looked over his shoulder, shot him a look, and walked away after two departing words. "She is." He knew his warning had been heard.

For the longest time, Theta Corps had been off the radars of other agencies. Now, they knew of them and since then things had been getting difficult. People in congress wanted oversight and to have their fingers in the pie. He wasn't about to hand over control to some fatass who spent his days in sessions and screwing his assistant behind his wife's back. *Not going to happen.*

Now, all he had to do was track Anabelle Lee down and convince her to come back to Theta Corps and him.

Chapter Fourteen

Kissing the stock of her MP-5, Anabelle Lee slung it over her shoulder and jogged to the end of the plane's ramp. It was pretty impressive feat considering she'd had to have the medic put in ten stitches on the outside of her thigh.

"Would you like a moment alone with that?" Ethan moved into her peripheral vision.

"I've had plenty of moments alone with this baby. That's why I survived *and* why I'm keeping it." She touched the healing bruise on her face and pasted a smile there as her brother neared.

"And here I thought we would have to rescue you."

"For a few moments, I thought you might as well. I'm happy to say you didn't, but I can't thank you enough for being there just in case I would have needed it."

He draped an arm around her and kissed her uninjured cheek. "I wasn't about to go tell Grams something happened to you. Maybe now you'll stick with the ones you know have your back."

"Can we not talk about my shitty track record with trusting men in either personal or work-related situations?" Though she tried to keep her tone light, she could hear the hint of pain that gave her away.

It sucked. Carlos then the fucking CIA.

"There's one that worked."

That voice. Hell, that man. She glanced ahead away from her brother and spied Masters standing there, dressed in a suit, the light gray shirt unbuttoned around his neck. The shimmering deep blue suit coat and pants fit him in ways that should have been illegal.

Damn it all. She had missed him.

To be honest, she'd not expected to see him again. Ever. Not after the night in his office. Sure, there were things she wished she could have said and told him, but time hadn't been on her side. Especially not when she had been fighting for her life to get out of the shithole country she'd been left in.

Now here he stood, right before her. *You can tell him everything you wanted to say beforehand.* Well, some things were easier than others. Her mouth clammed up and she could only swallow as she looked at him and drank in his vision.

She propped a hand against her hip and stared as he approached. His stride was a sure, confident, masculine one she was happy to watch year-round. She brushed some hair away from her face as the wind whipped it.

"I don't know. There's been issues with them all."

He slowed before her. "Aren't there issues with all relationships?"

"All mine." She adjusted the strap on her MP-5 and watched his eyes light up.

"There's one that would like another shot."

She shook her head, too exhausted to go down that road yet again. Her brain screamed at her that this was the chance she'd just finished saying she wished she'd been able to have.

"What for?"

He reached out and stroked a hand down her bruise, his touch as tender as any ever had the right to be. She leaned into his touch before she recovered and drew away.

"Because I realized I don't want to do this without you."

She crossed her arms. "This something you want to do in front of my brother?"

Masters never looked away from her. "I don't give a damn who I do it in front of. This has nothing to do with them. This is our business, Annie. Yours and mine. No one else's."

Damn him for calling me Annie. I don't need to be swayed any more in his favor.

"So talk."

What difference did it make if they were on a large tarmac with planes coming and going? So what if there were men going up into the belly of the transport that had just brought her home and taking off skid loads with forklifts?

The Masters she knew kept everything contained, tight and to the chest.

"Fine." He stepped flush to her, close enough if she took a deep breath her chest would brush his, yet he left space between them. As if to taunt her. It worked. "When I heard what the CIA did, I was pissed. I'd been trying to get in touch with you for months, no way of knowing where you were or if you were even okay. Then I learn you were disavowed."

She shrugged. "So you wanted to rush to my rescue? It happens. It was the damn CIA."

His smile made her knees weak and her heart nearly jump out of her chest. "Of course, I did, but I know you. You don't need me to rescue you. You don't need anyone to rescue you."

Somehow, he shifted closer and the wind brought his subtle masculine scent to her nose, erasing the smell of jet fuel and her own stench.

"Didn't stop me from wanting to, but I figured I could do more for you on this end and went to make sure if for some reason you weren't as good as I knew you are, your grandmother wouldn't want for anything. I also told them to stay the fuck away from you."

"You threatened the CIA?"

His shrug was lazy, showing his lack of concern. "They're not allowed to operate on this soil. Besides, I'll put up my company to theirs any day."

"Why are you telling me all this?"

"Because I want you to know, I've figured it out."

She blinked, confused. "Figured what out?"

"What my life needs."

"And that would be?"

"It needs a feisty, redheaded woman in it who doesn't allow me to get away with any shit. Calls me to the mat when I need it, hell, even when I don't think I need it."

"So buy your girlfriend a red wig."

"Wouldn't do me a damn bit of good for the attitude. I need that around me. I need *you* around me, Anabelle Lee."

She flicked her tongue along her lips, desperate not to cave and launch into his arms, allowing him to hold her. "And, what, I'm supposed to sit at home like a dutiful wife while you continue to run Theta Corps?"

"Hell, no. I want you back. I want you at my side for business and life."

Warmth sprang up from her toes and spilled throughout her entire body. "We butt heads."

He nodded and pursed his kissable lips. "No argument here. But we're good for each other. You make me want to be better, do better."

"What happens the next time I have to wear something revealing and am in danger?"

Masters leaned closer. "I don't promise to be cheerful about it, but I'll keep my mouth shut and let you do what you do so fucking well. I'm sorry about my behavior, Anabelle Lee. I know I have no right to tell you what to wear or question your work ethic and how you're going about doing a job. We can keep work, work. I want to know at the end of the day, at the end of any mission, you're coming home with me."

"Anything else you want to say?"

He frowned. "What else is there?"

"For fuck's sake, man, you need to tell her you love her!"

The combined cry came from the belly of the plane and the men who were up there working.

He looked back at her and smiled wryly. "Well, yes, there is that."

She couldn't stop her answering grin. "There is, huh?"

Masters wrapped his arms around her waist and dragged her that last bit of distance that had been between them so they now touched.

"Definitely. But they're right. I've not told you. I love you, Annie. Have since soon after I met you. I will do my best to not only keep you safe, but support you in whatever you want to do. I want the chance to spend the rest of my life with you."

Anabelle Lee pushed up on the toes of her combat boots and pressed her lips to his. He opened his mouth under her slight pressure and met her tongue with his own. They tangled and twisted with each other as she wound her arms around his neck, dragging his fingers through his hair. It didn't matter how mad she was with him — this was the one man for her. No one else did for her as he did. And no one would.

Epilogue

She exhaled slowly and inched her way down the darkened hallway. Before the corner, she paused and counted, low and slow until she knew the cameras wouldn't be on her trajectory.

Anabelle Lee slipped into her destination and made her way to the back of the room to wait. She didn't have long before the door swung open and her target stepped in, laughing at something he'd said to someone in the hall.

She waited as he sat, opened his desk and reached into the drawer to pour himself a drink from the scotch he pulled out. She stepped up behind him and settled the muzzle of her SIG against his neck.

"I truly dislike being hung out to dry when it's one of yours who is the traitor. Do you know what it's like on Rendova or any of the other islands I had to swim to and try to stay alive until I was rescued?"

Shady jumped and the glass in his hand tumbling to the desk. She rolled her eyes. *How the hell do the CIA operate if their men are this easy to sneak up on?*

"It was nothing personal," he said. "Work. You know how it goes."

"Nothing personal?" She slid the muzzle back and forth along the skin. "You didn't want someone to work for you on an even-keel basis. You wanted someone who had the training, but wasn't on anyone's radar for them to lure out your mole. And if, no, when shit hit the fan, you wouldn't need to explain to anyone about your fuck up. You knew he was bad. You *knew* he was going to betray whomever was with him that time. Tell me I'm wrong."

He shifted to the left and she clucked her tongue, tapping his left shoulder with a second weapon.

"Let's not make any jumpy movements, I'd really hate to kill you so soon."

"I'm a CIA agent. You can't kill me and get away with it."

She leaned closer to his ear. "Your mistake from the start was assuming you knew just what I could and couldn't do. I could put two right here and be gone before anyone knew better. No prints, no name — remember, you haven't ever heard of me."

"I would just prefer you didn't kill him, Anabelle Lee."

She swore under her breath and cut her gaze to the right, where Masters stepped into view.

"What are you doing here?"

Masters moved to her side and took her weapons away from Shady. "Taking you away."

"I'm going to make you —"

Anabelle Lee watched Masters punch him in the jaw and send him spiraling off his chair to the floor.

She looked up at the man who owned her heart. "Seriously? You punched him?"

He shrugged and pulled her closer. "You had not one, but two weapons on him, Annie."

"He betrayed *me*. I don't know what you're so pissed off about."

"He endangered you." Masters kissed her. "And it pisses me off."

"I don't think I should be here when he wakes up."

"Up to the roof. The chopper is there."

"How do you have a helicopter here?"

"I'm the head of a top government agency. It's not uncommon for us to visit other agencies."

She crossed her arms. "And so you just happened to have a meeting here tonight?"

"Perks of being the boss. Come on, Annie. Let's go."

She shook her head and said, "I'll meet you up there." With a single look at him, she slipped out the way she'd come in.

* * * *

Masters stared at the woman sleeping on the bed in the middle of the hut. It had been the only way to keep her to himself without interruptions. He'd whisked her away to a deserted island that had the minimum of things.

There wasn't going to be a five-star resort for them — in those places were phones and other people. Here he had her to himself and that was how he wanted it. They were surrounded by crystalline-blue waters.

He walked over the floor and sank beside her, reaching out to brush her hair away, exposing her spine. Bending down, he pressed light kisses to her creamy skin, which was for once free of any bruising or other injury.

She shifted on the smooth, cool, blue cotton sheets but didn't wake. He dragged his fingers along her side and over the soft curve of her buttocks, until he reached the back of her knee. A slow moan slid from her throat and she spread her legs.

The temptation was too much for him. He ran his hand up her other leg until he reached the juncture of her thighs. He bit his lower lip as he ran his finger between her cleft. She lifted slightly from the mattress.

He rubbed it again. And again.

Her moans grew as he pushed two fingers inside her heat. Hell, he was ready to heft her up on her knees and drive his cock deep inside her until she screamed his name. Readjusting, he kissed his way back to her ass and placed to tiny nips on her cheeks.

"Masters," she rumbled, pushing back into her hand. "While I love waking this way, I need you to fuck me."

He bit her ass again, harder, loving the jump. "Not yet. This is my time."

Angling around, he settled between her legs, still moving his fingers within her. He used his shoulders to spread her legs farther apart. Her scent filled his nostrils and he clenched back a growl of pure lust.

He drew her up and began licking her pussy around his plunging digits. Her moans increased as her hips moved.

"Shit," she cried. "Masters, I fucking need you."

Words he'd never tire of hearing. He drew on her clit and added another finger to her pussy.

"Fuck, yeah," she hollered, bunching the sheets in her hands.

His cock pushed hard against his pants. Lifting up, he shrugged out of them and grasped his dick. He ran it along her slit and pulled away his fingers before putting the head right there.

"Yes," she begged.

"I love you, Annie," he said, slipping into her with a single smooth stroke.

"Love you, too, Masters."

Her back bowed as he thrust within her. He gripped her hips and powered hard, needing everything she gave and more. He asked, she gave. Her head was on the mattress, her ass was up in the air and he put one hand on the small of her back, not that he needed to keep her there, but he liked to have her skin beneath his palm.

Hours later, they lay in the same bed. He had her in his arms and his eyes closed as they watched the sky change to beautiful shades of rich golds, oranges, purples and more as the sun took itself to bed. As they lay there, he played with the strap of her halter-top dress. The warm breeze made the sheet over them barely necessary.

She yawned and reclined closer to him. "When do we have to go back to the real world?"

"When do you want to go?"

"I don't. Not for a while. I get you and no distractions all to myself. Why would I want to give that up?"

"I think your grandmother would like you to come back at some point. Not to mention, Beau and Ethan." He picked some of her hair and ran it though his fingers. "Personally, I like having you to myself, as well."

She rolled toward him and gave him a smile he'd come to enjoy all too much. "If we can't just stay here forever, then I guess we should make the best of the time we have left."

Masters held her on top of him, cock thick and ready again. "I couldn't have said it better myself."

They stayed for a week and as they flew back to the States, he got a call.

"Masters."

He looked in time to see Anabelle Lee striding from the back, dressed in her utilities and armed to the teeth. She braided her hair as she approached.

How the fuck does she do that?

He ended the call and she sat on the seat opposite him. "What's up? Where are we going?"

"We've got a lead on General Otman."

Her lips turned up in a feral grin. "Good, been waiting for this for a while."

Less than twenty-four hours since they had left their private island paradise, Masters watched the love of his life stride down the steps of his private jet to meet her brother and cousin.

She looked at him, winked and turned back to her family as they piled into a rundown truck and drove off into the African landscape. Moments later, he was ascending once more into the sky as his pilot headed them home. On his seat was a note.

Opening it, he smiled as her handwriting jumped out at him.

I go to work, but when I come home, it's to you.
~Annie

"Damn straight, you will."

He reached for his phone and began patching in those he needed for this op to be a success, not worried about her safety more than usual. She knew how to handle herself and she was back with Beau and Ethan.

He'd see her soon enough.

Masters couldn't stop watching the clock, counting down the minutes until he would lay eyes on Anabelle Lee once more. She'd been gone far too long this time. He stared at the papers on his desk, requisitions for needed items. Things he didn't give a damn about.

His secretary had gone, he was the only one there when the phone rang. "Masters," he barked after punching the speaking phone button.

"Harper from the NSA."

Placing his pen down, he lifted the receiver. "What can I do for you, Harper from the NSA?"

A few short finger clicks and the man's dossier sat before his eyes on the computer screen. As Harper talked, Masters read and listened. When the man mentioned Tajikistan, he stopped reading.

That was where he'd sent his team on their most recent mission. Where he'd sent Anabelle Lee.

Leaning back in his chair, Masters steepled his fingers and listened.

"I know technically, and of course officially, the US can't operate in that country over there. We have heard rumors you may have some assets over there."

"Why would I have assets where they can't be? Isn't operating in secrecy your company's MO?"

"And Theta Corps doesn't work in the dark? You're not exactly know for following the rules. There's talk about your company."

Neither here nor there. "Because there are *never* rumors floating around DC," he drolled. "You seem to be playing some sort of game. Fishing for information and doing a piss-poor job of it, if I do say so myself. I've never been good at these things, so let me put this out there. I do not have anyone in Tajikistan. You may want to check with your source and get on them about spreading such rumors."

"We have satellite images of a redheaded woman."

He smiled. *So do I.*

Anabelle Lee strolled into the room, fresh off the plane. Side arms strapped to each dark material-covered thigh blended in with her BDUs. Her dark gray shirt hid none of her curves.

"So? There are plenty of redheads in the world. And there are wigs for people to use if they so desire."

Anabelle Lee cocked an eyebrow at him but didn't speak. His woman had returned. He wanted off this phone call so he could welcome her home properly.

Her red hair was forward over one shoulder in a tight braid. She had a panda skullcap on the top of her head. No dark streaks on her creamy skin for camouflage. She was gorgeous, despite the exhaustion on her face.

She paused by his desk and sat on the corner, one leg dangling back and forth. Masters wanted to touch her but knew he had to finish up his call first.

"I have your word on that?"

He shrugged. "Absolutely. I don't have anyone over there." He hung up the phone without another word. Wheeling his chair around the corner, he reached for his woman then drew her onto his lap.

"Hey, there," she whispered, looping her arms around his neck. "I missed you."

"Likewise, Annie."

He kissed her, wrapping her tight in his embrace. "Ready to go home?" he asked when he managed to break free of her luscious mouth.

"Whose?"

He paused. They both had their own spaces, but he wanted more than the casual boyfriend-girlfriend arrangement. He wanted husband and wife status with this woman.

"Come on," he said, getting to his feet and sliding her down his body.

"Where are we going?" She landed lightly on the balls of her feet.

"I'm marrying you."

She blinked, froze, and stared at him. "What?"

He took a second to run it over in his head, how it must have sounded to her. Definitely not the best delivery he could have come with, and sure as hell wasn't how he'd planned it in his head all those times he'd practiced his proposal. But it was out now and he sure as fuck wasn't taking it back.

He swallowed. "I want to marry you, Anabelle Lee."

"Now?" she asked. "In this?" She gestured to her clothing.

"I don't give a fuck what you wear. You can pick a bedsheet if you want. But yes, now."

She crossed her arms. "We can't marry tonight."

He grabbed his phone. "Why not?"

"It's after ten at night, Masters. No one is going to marry us."

"They will in Vegas." He shoved his hand in his pocket. "Wheels up in twenty, DeWayne. Vegas is the destination."

Anabelle Lee reached out to him. "Why are you doing this?"

"I told you," he said, replacing the receiver. "I want to marry you. Now. Tonight. And if it means misappropriating the use of the company jet, then so be it. I want to lay my head down tonight with a wife beside me."

She stepped closer to him and walked her fingers up his chest. "Not the most romantic proposal I've heard, but it damn sure is the best one I've ever received. Yes, I'll marry you, Masters. Tonight."

He claimed her mouth once more. They could figure out the big family wedding later—right now, this was for them, and them alone.

About the Author

Aliyah Burke is an avid reader and is never far from pen and paper (or the computer). She is married to a career military man, and they have a German Shepherd, two Borzois, and a DSH cat. Her days are spent sharing her time between work, writing, and dog training.

Aliyah loves to hear from readers.

You can find her contact information, website details and author profile page at http://www.totallybound.com.